HAIL CHANTER

**Books
by
Gerald Hausman**

GUNS
Turtle Dream
Ghost Walk
Tunkashila

STAR SONG *series*
Evil Chasing Way
Hand Trembler
Sungazer
Hail Chanter

For more information
visit: www.SpeakingVolumes.us

HAIL CHANTER

GERALD HAUSMAN

SPEAKING VOLUMES, LLC
NAPLES, FLORIDA
2024

Hail Chanter

Copyright © 2024 by Gerald Hausman

Drawings by Mariah Fox Copyright © 2024

All rights reserved. No part of this book may be reproduced or transmitted in any form or by any means without written permission.

ISBN 979-8-89022-232-9

For Jay DeGroat and family
and
Ray Brown and family

Acknowledgments

Thanks to Scott Momaday and Tony Hillerman for inspiration. Special thanks to Anais Savariau for scans. Thanks to Mariah Fox for the historical Native line drawings.

The Song of the Hail Chanter

In the beginning
there was no sun
and no one knew
night from day
or day from night

So the first people
made a round sun
with a turquoise face.

This sun was painted
in sand, and from
that time to this time

There has been

Morning light
Midday light
Evening light

and the twelve threads
of Dark-light-Night

One

Lightning

I died today.
 Or maybe yesterday.
 I can't be sure.
 All I know is that I am now alive and lying in a hospital bed. The nurse tells me I was hit by lightning.
 She takes my temperature and my pulse. The next thing I know I am swimming in a glitter of haze that begins to darken, and keeps darkening, until it is darker than dark, and I am unconscious.
 Dead or alive,
 I am Some One
 Some Body
 Some Where.
 Then my eyes open into the world of Lightning.
 The nurse is dressed in green.
 "Who are you?" I ask.
 "I am the one trying to save your life. Who are you?"
 On this question, I am not sure.
 Am I the one I have been studying in my Navajo Mythology course?
 Am I the legendary younger brother named T*obachischin* who was killed by lightning and brought back to life? My mind begins to spool like a fishing reel, sending me into another world. I am one of the Hero Twins my professor has told us about.

Gerald Hausman

My elder brother, *Nayenezgani*,
always carries a dark staff and now he comes in search of me.
With lightning flashing before him
and behind him, he comes with a
rock crystal into which he talks.
I can hear him in my dream brain.

Through the two blue earths I hear
him coming.

Does he know I also have lightning in me?

Somehow, I believe I am in the
place of yellow earths …

                ***

Yet things outside me have changed.
I am now beyond yellow earth.
I am in the place of white earth.

If only I could see Elder Brother's dark
staff it would help me place myself where
I am supposed to be.

A clue, I can hear his staff thumping.
I can also hear his lightning crackling.

And now I can see him moving through
two blue woods and beyond into

Hail Chanter

yellow woods, and then white
woods where I see the lightning
flashing before him and behind
him.

He comes through the place of
two blue mosses. Farther on
he comes through three yellow mosses,
and beyond, farther beyond that,
the place of four white mosses where I
have been struck by lightning.

From the Emergence Place,
Nayenezgani, my older brother,
swings his dark staff to control
the lightning. He has protection
I didn't have when the lightning
broke me and left me
lifeless—am I dead now?
I really don't know.

Nayenezgani awakens me with
a rainbow that he carries like a bow
in his left hand while whirling
his protective dark staff
to ward off his own encircling
lightning.

Suddenly he awakens me.
"I carry you, *Tobachischin*, up

the ladder of life. Can you hear
me?"

I tell him, "Yes." It is all I can
manage to say. It takes great
effort to speak.

But *Nayenezgani's* rainbow is helping me see,
as it lifts me up and carries me from the
broken shards of my lightning-crushed
body into the upper level of the rainbow.

Nayenezgani carries me up the ladder's
first rung.
Farther up, I see the ladder's
second rung.
Farther up from there, the ladder's third
rung.
Farther, and still higher, *Nayenezgani*
carries me up the ladder's fourth
rung. He is the carrier, but the rainbow ladder
is helping him.

In this way we go up until
We are above Emergence Mountain.
From there he carries me
to Chief Mountain, Rain Mountain,
Corn Mountain, Pollen Mountain,
Corn Beetle Mountain.

Hail Chanter

My eyes are fully open now.
My ears are open, too.
I hear little chickadees singing.
The lightnings are all gone.
Only a rainbow-bow of *Nayenezgani*
lights my way.

I hear a voice from Old Age Hogan.
It says, "This is your home, too,
Grandchild."

Nayenezgani is gone. Old Grandfather sits
down beside me. "We sit upon a
pollen dancer," he says.

Then he tells me,
"Your legs are yours again
Your body is yours again
Your mind is yours again
Your voice is yours again
Your powers are all yours again."

Then, "You, my grandson, are
Hail Chanter, long lived and
strong. Blessed has your life
become: and all that is blessed
behind you, below you, above you
and all around you. All this is blessed
again by me, for you are
Hail Chanter."

Two

Long Walk Home

Grandfather pointed to the earth.

"This is where we go. Our homeward journey begins here, Grandson."

I looked down at the small hole made by a ground squirrel.

"How could we fit into such a tiny hole?"

"Watch, and you will see."

He raised his walking-stick, and I watched as the stick pointed downward.

Grandfather smiled. "We will follow our cousin, Ground Squirrel," he said.

Then he began to blow into the small dark cavity. He did four, deep distinct breaths. And as I looked on, the squirrel hole widened, opened. It grew great in size, turning into a man-sized tunnel.

"Go ahead, Grandson. The way is clear now."

Carefully, I eased myself in. As I did so, pebbles and dirt dropped on my head. Grandfather followed. More dirt came down.

Below my feet, nothing but darkness.

"Keep going, Grandson. Use your back to steady yourself and with your hands, take hold of the roots."

I did as he told me.

Soon I saw a wink of light below my feet. Tiny pebbles from Grandfather's feet rained down on me.

Now I saw that the ground squirrel's hole was fully open. And I saw that we were in a cave and could walk upright.

After a little while the cave turned into a wide ledge of stone. Down below, the silver gleam of an arroyo flashed.

It wasn't long before we stopped and drank from that ribbon of water. The damp sand was covered with animal tracks.

"Give thanks, Grandson. Sing with me." He sang a whisper prayer low into the wind, and I followed him. Then he made a fine circle of cornmeal pollen which he kept in his medicine bag. We sang together again.

It was strange but even in this desolate empty canyon, I felt eyes upon us.

"Does anyone live here?" I asked.

"Animals and men live everywhere," he said.

He raised his walking-stick.

It quivered in the cedar gloom and showed us the way up the canyon.

We walked then on the tops of rocks, not in the water or damp sand.

The crickets spoke to us, and then, as we came near, they silenced themselves in the water willows. A chill wind came from afar.

I looked up and saw a red-shouldered hawk.

"He is telling us," Grandfather said, "that there are two-leggeds up ahead."

A teasing draft of piñon smoke whispered in the wind, and because we were in such a deep canyon, darkness came soon.

I heard voices close by.

Grandfather dipped into his medicine bag and sprinkled some dust on my head and shoulders.

"This is a gift from Owl Boy. No one can see us now." After sprinkling himself with Owl Boy's medicine, we continued to walk, and now, even the night-dark crickets softened their song and paid no attention to us.

Somewhere close by, a small owl hooted once, twice, then two more times.

Grandfather spoke a soft prayer to Owl Boy. I felt Owl Boy's spirit follow us into the firelit cover of a camp of men. Some were crouched, their wide straw hats pulled low. Others were curled up on their sides under banded serape blankets.

We walked into their camp, glancing neither right nor left.

Two night-guards were talking softly. They had rifles in the crooks of their arms. There was a clay whiskey jug between them.

The hunter's moon was high on the canyon rim. There was meat roasting on iron spikes. These two men were eating and drinking, and Grandfather walked up to the fire and stood for a moment, waiting for Owl Boy's message. One hoot was all that came. Grandfather waited for three more that didn't come. The guards continued to talk and joke as Grandfather walked silently up to the fire and cut a large slice of roasted meat.

He returned to where I was waiting for him. We walked in silence under the high yellow moon but when we reached the top of the hill that led out of the arroyo, I heard a whining sound. Someone was shooting arrows, not aiming, as I could see, but …

Suddenly, a *thunk* as a hunting arrow lodged itself in Grandfather's chest. At the same time, an owl flew low over our heads, making no noise but the gentle wind on its wings.

Back in the camp, I heard voices.

Grandfather, by then, sank to his knees. "I am dead, a *chindi*, Grandson. Go ahead without me. I will follow your tracks." His eyes closed. He leaned forward a little, I caught him with both arms. "They can see into invisibility," he whispered.

He sighed once and was gone.

Hail Chanter

By now, I could hear the hunter coming as branches of wind-pines bumped against his chest.

"Over here," the hunter called. More men were coming.

I could do nothing now but run, and that I did, as fast as I could. While I ran in the canyon moonlight, I sang my own Owl Song.

Owl Boy,
You who sits on feather pine
You with white smoke for feather
You with curved claws
You who always offers help
To those in need,
Why did you abandon us
On this night?

I ran on light feet of moonlight crying hot tears but knowing Grandfather was with me. Probably just up ahead, trackless and invisible, yet ever protective of me. He would not go on the Journey North, the place where the Dead live, until he knew that I was safe.

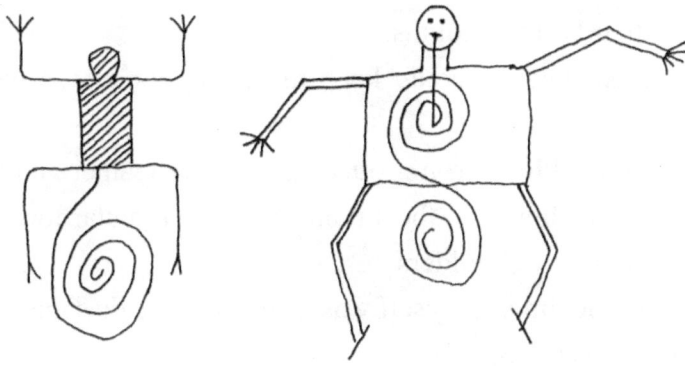

Three

Race Against the Whirlwind

I counted my blessings as I ran.

I had Grandfather's medicine bag. I had his knife. I had the water pouch he made of otter skin, and it was still half-full of water.

I counted myself lucky. I had no idea what lay before me. But I ran on in the night dark.

Then I heard Grandfather's voice.

"Do not fear the Whirlwind. Like the desert, Grandchild, you are a thing of permanence. Keep running, don't stop. Fear nothing."

Soon after, the Whirlwinds multiplied. Great capes of dust and when they joined, they became one.

They moaned as they devoured the desert. I glanced over my right shoulder as I ran, and I saw them eating up cactus arms and tumbleweeds, piñon trees and fanged yuccas.

I kept on but I could see they were gaining on me. They were four giant snakes twined into one. Four circular winds sucking small songbirds into their hollow mouths.

I was next unless I could keep my pace, but it was wearing me down.

I saw a great blue heron ground into bits of feather and bone. One of its wings was flung into the air, and by some circular force, it landed momentarily on my shoulders.

At that same time, I, myself was thrust into the dust-pierced air and given a winged chance.

I flew.

The ghostly growls of the whirlwinds fell behind me.

Now the lightnings came back. Bolts of blue and white fire. I covered my ears as I ran.

Then, as quickly as it had grown from nothing, the growling, screaming winds went back to nothing.

The sudden silence was now broken only by needle-like sand crystals, and I heard the raven's cough. A fox barking. An eagle cry.

I pulled myself forward. I was breathless, starved for air, suffocating.

That was when the whirlwind came back and pounced and crushed me to the earth.

At the same time, it began to snow. I felt the sting of tiny ice crystals. The brown desert ground was muffled with them. It was suddenly white all around me.

But I hung in the air, hung there in the crippling grip of the whirlwind.

I was knocked about, punched blind by them, but then I found Grandfather's walking-stick. "Beat the paws of the whirlwind. You have possession of my magic stick. Use it now."

I did as he said. The walking-stick made an unearthly sound. A terrible high-piercing scream in my head.

I fell to the earth and crawled under a great white rock.

I felt the ice-cold silver snow on my chest.

I felt the wet leather deerskin of Grandfather's medicine bag. Fumbling, I grabbed his arrow-straightener.

The moment I had it, I felt saved.

The whirlwinds claws melted, the snow stopped, the wind died, I was home again in Grandfather's arms.

And I heard his voice. "Remember, Grandson, you are also the Sun's son."

Hearing his words, I began to sing the spirit-strengthening song that Grandfather taught me.

I am the Sun's son.
I sit upon a turquoise horse
At the opening of the sky
My horse walks on terrifying hooves
And stands on the upper
Circle of the rainbow
With a sunbeam for a bridle
My horse circles all the people
Of the earth, and he is mine
Tomorrow he will belong
To another

After I sang this song, I no longer felt weak. I had beaten the evil teeth of a killing winter wind.

If someone, or something, wished to finish me off, they would have to do better than this. For I had Grandfather's walking stick and Sun Father's turquoise horse, and I was alive.

Four

Beautiful Woman

Dawn came as it does with four fingers of color. I did a blessing of corn pollen from Grandfather's medicine bag. I moved my feet in the four directions, facing East first and singing to the dawn. Out of which walked a beautiful woman I had not seen before.

She stepped out of the darkness wrapped in white fur of fox. When she saw how poorly I was clothed and how ragged I looked, she sprinkled some little grains on my shoulders from her medicine pouch.

"These are my gift to you," she said, "they came to me from Changing Woman, Mother Earth." Then she gave me a small bundle of woven feathers.

"This should improve your looks," she added.

I put the sacred blanket over my shoulders. The moment I did so, Beautiful Woman reached out her hands and both of us were lifted into the air.

Then, as we soared through the sky, I noticed that Beautiful Woman's dress was made from white butterflies while my blanket was woven from red and black woodpecker feathers.

The sky turned light as we went higher. Lightning lashed it North, South, East and West, but somehow didn't touch us.

"You needn't be scared. Lightning won't harm you," Beautiful Woman said.

"How do you know?"

She withdrew a zigzag lightning stick from the rainbow-colored band at her waist.

"This *Ketahn* is our protector," she told me.

We rose higher until we were in the star family known as Dipper. She never let go of my hand and though Lightning whip-cracked around us it also got fainter, and finally faded.

Then Gray Heron flew up from behind us.

"You must be the wanderers I've heard of. So, you should know there is a wicked white bird named *Tsin-trah-ilkai.* He has blue wings and a sharp black and white beak. We should return to earth now. Follow me."

As we got closer to earth, it began to rain and Lightning returned. Great arrows of molten heat flamed the sky.

I could barely see Beautiful Woman. The Lightning was that bright and hot.

Then, at the same time we drifted down toward earth, a storm of birds surrounded us.

"Those birds are another kind of Lightning, don't let them touch you or you will be burned to death," said Gray Heron. "We are now almost down to *Yah-hahoh-kah*, the hole through the sky. When you touch the earth, look for a bird, a snake or toad. If you see one, sprinkle corn pollen on it, from Grandfather's medicine bag. Then Lightning will not touch you."

We touched the sand soon after Gray Heron melted away in the sky.

A crooked snake, it seemed, awaited us. Beautiful Woman and I sprinkled corn pollen on the snake and then, even though Lightning was striking all around us, and blinding our eyes with cruel light, we felt nothing but warm summer air.

At last, we were home.

Five

Little Wind

All this time, I'd been eating on the run. Sometimes wild onions, sometimes the roots of river plants. Once I stumble upon the little dark beans favored by the *bilagaana*. The ones you boil and make into a hot dark drink that takes away hunger. For a long while I gnawed on the shank bone Grandfather had pulled from the killers' fire.

Once I ate wild grass seeds and wood rats, burned corn from an ancient field and rotted peaches from another. I sucked on burnt cobs found in an old fire pit.

Beautiful Woman encouraged me to eat cornflower pollen as she did. She showed me a bee's nest in the burl of an oak. I ate handfuls of honey, and my hands and chest were sticky from it.

One day she said, "Where are we going?" And I heard Grandfather's voice in the snail shell of my ear, "Tell her you are going somewhere far to the North."

She worried about my hair. Along with the sticky honey, the smoke, the afterburn smell of Lightning, my hair needed combing, so she washed it with yucca suds made from the plant's bulbs. Then she combed it in the sun with a porcupine comb and braided and tied it with a strand of doeskin. She, too, had a medicine bag with great tools in it.

So, with clean shining hair we listened to the wood doves warbling and cooing in the twilight. I stared at my bare feet. They resembled old beaten leather. My legs were also scarred from Lightning.

Before the risen dawn, Beautiful Woman flew off into the tamarisk forest. When she returned, her arms were bundled with yucca leaves. I watched her as she wove me a new pair of sandals.

That afternoon, she said, as we walked toward the North, "It will be better if we keep to the mountains."

Suddenly, a swirl of yellow warblers came song-whipping out of the Wind.

"This is a sign," she said.

Then quail drummed up out of the sagebrush with snap-popping wings.

Sheets of orange flame rose out of the horizon. The wind battered the scrub pines. I could feel the heat on my skin as the pines boomed into flame.

That was when Beautiful Woman told me to climb on her back.

At the same time she flew us high above the earth-torment below.

Grandfather spoke into my inner ear. "Come back to earth now and let *Niltsi*, Little Wind, carry you to safety. You must not use all the power in Beautiful Woman's wings. You will need it in days to come. Don't worry, I will be there for both of you. But you must remember that soon I will go through the great hole in the rock of the North.

That night we could see the mountains. Behind us the firestorm still danced. Yet now came a rusty red rain. The angry fire hissed and spit like Great Snake.

Then we saw who was chasing us. Four giant black horses, ridden by four ghostly *chindi* riders.

They came crashing out of the clouds, plunging down upon us. It was like Grandfather told me when I was very little— "When the earth is angry dark things come out of the sky."

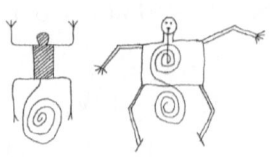

Six

White Light

We traveled to the Blue Lukachukai mountains and from there Grandfather told me to go to Crown Point.

Beautiful Woman followed but as the hours went by, her white butterfly cape began unraveling in the hot sun and she herself got fainter until, finally, she was but a vision. Merely a mist of butterfly magic; then even less than that – a cape of disappearing smoke.

"You must be careful not to get too close to the hole that leads into the afterworld," Grandfather whispered into my ear.

I did what he said.

I was standing back from the night wind hole, and I watched as he entered—I couldn't see him, but I could feel him leaving my inner ear and going into the darkness.

But once he was in the hole and then on the other side of it, I could see him as he once was, a man. Then he was gone in the mist.

I then stood in the soundless emptiness of silence itself, and only Little Wind, *Niltsi,* stayed behind to keep me standing upright.

Well, I was wrong about that too. One white butterfly fluttered into my face. Then she was gone. Then, Beautiful Woman was gone and I was alone.

My guardians were gone, I was alone and lost. Even to myself. Alone in the world, whatever world it was, and whatever person I was.

So, you could say, I died today.

Or maybe it was yesterday.

I don't know for sure.

If time passed, I did not know it.

All I knew was that I suddenly woke in a hospital bed.
A nurse told me I'd been struck by lightning.
"Who's the Green Hornet?" she asked.

Seven

Cow Creek Blessing

It has been a month and a half. No, it has been two whole months. Or so I have been told.

I am talking about the weeks of daily radiation treatments. I am almost done with them. Almost free again. The Hail Chanter is almost done with his song and his desire to cancel the memory of the Lightning strike.

It's almost over.

But we don't know for sure. There is no absolute with cancer. Which is why they call it the Big C.

Memory is a thing that pulls you back sometimes by force, other times by warmth and gentleness.

Laura says, "Do you remember the night in the Pecos wilderness?"

"You mean, the night on Cow Creek when Loren Straight Eagle Plume and I washed our hair using the crushed root of the yucca."

"What was it he called it in Navajo?"

"*Yay-bi-tsa-si.*"

In Spanish the translation is Lord's Candlestick or the "Light of Jesus," as I remembered.

"At night, in the flare of the fire you could make out dancers."

I told Laura, "I can still feel the cold creek water and the healing suds of the yucca."

I remembered it as if it were a day ago. Loren doing the blessing as we rubbed the medicine into our scalp. But only now does it come home to me that Loren was washing away the little ghost man in the canyon. He'd seen him, heard him speak. The little ghost who said he believed he'd betrayed his people by falling asleep when he was supposed to be guarding and protecting them.

This ceremony in the depths of the canyon—two men and a ghost, all three of them seeking salvation of different kinds. Forgiveness comes hard sometimes. If it comes at all. *Candelario Los Senores.*

Eight

The Mayan Dragon

Let me tell you about the healing lizard that was another version of Gila Monster. Bluejay came to see me as he always does. "It's the Mayan Dragon Lizard," he said, "they call it *Pichiquatay*."

He went on to explain: "They say there are two phases or forms of this creature. One is a healer; the other is a destroyer. One is a well-armed warrior. He can put people back together again when they have been crushed by accidents like your lightning strike that infused you with cancer."

That was, I remembered, the ancient Navajo ceremony of the *Flintway*. In this healing story, Elder Brother enters the place known as Earth Whirling.

"That is the place that is part of our Emergence from the underworld," Bluejay said. "It's a forbidden place for those of us not Navajo."

"Isn't it true, Bluejay?" I asked.

"What is true?"

"That lightning can cause cancer?"

"You can be shattered by Lightning, but I don't know for sure about cancer, although, I, for one, believe they are related."

"Just like it happened to me," I added.

"I know what the white doctors say about that," Bluejay said. Then he added, "You know the story. How Elder Brother was saved and pieced together again. Thunder, Lightning and Rainbow gave him powers and Elder Brother was whole. After which he was healed by Black Ant and Spider. The ant carried the little parts of the broken Brother;

Spider wove together happiness-healing, walking in harmony, and glittering. That is how Elder Brother came back to life using all of those healing people."

"What is the lesson in all of that?"

Bluejay said, "The lesson is stay on the path of wellness, righteousness, and beauty."

I have followed his wise words. But sometimes wellness and illness get confused. We think we are well when we are ill.

As for the Mayan mystery lizard, he broke out of his confinement, he went elsewhere, and was never seen again by me. So I suppose, I healed myself. And sometimes, I feel my joined bones singing. Other times those same bones feel heated, as if in a stove.

Nine

Guardian

My storyteller friend, Ramon told me about how he was crawling through a cave when his hand met a century old, mud-daubed wall. His mother, the healer, had warned him of the creatures, the gods of the dreamtime. "Some of them," she said, are spirits and they can help you when you're in trouble. Other times they cause confusion because of their powers."

"I know of them," I told Ramon.

He went on with his story.

"My hand," Ramon told me, "reached out in the darkness. I could see nothing but night."

"I could feel the hand, very cold. it was. It touched my own. I felt its power immediately."

"What did it feel like beyond the coldness?" I asked him.

"Palm on palm," he answered.

"Someone was there with you?"

Ramon said, "No, it wasn't like that. I was all alone. Something was in the cave with me but I didn't know exactly what it was."

I said, "The same thing happened to me."

"The unseen guardian?" he asked.

He smiled. "It is strange to feel safe in the hand of a spirit. A ghost."

"I know that feeling. That's what happened to me in the hospital."

For a time, we both sat in silence, thinking and remembering.

Then, he went on.

"It was the sound of dry bells. The hand in the dark cave. And it was like that hand was talking to me with a voice of dry bells."

I shook my head. "I've never heard those bells."

"When I first heard them," he said, "I thought they were outside of the cave. Maybe some small oak tree tapping against a rock. But that wasn't it. The dry bells were a different kind of spirit voice. When I backed slowly out of the cave, they stopped ringing. And I heard only the desert wind."

"What were those bells?"

"A very large rattlesnake, I think, only inches from my face."

His face tightened for a moment. Then he sang this song:

Palm to palm
The hand
Made of mud
Belonged to
The cave's
Long gone
Guardian
I was safe, held
In the grasp
Of a being
Who was
No longer
Flesh and blood

Ten

Sky Gods

After a while friends came to my house in Tesuque almost every week. Every one of them was a storyteller. And they knew of my devotion to stories of ghosts, gods, and spirits who would come when I most needed them, which, since my lightning strike, was almost all the time now.

"They are everywhere," Bluejay said. He was my oldest Navajo friend because he was a roommate of mine back in college in the early sixties.

Now he had come back to me when I was in the hospital. Bluejay usually took a long time telling a story, which he didn't call a story because, to him, it was just a conversation.

He began very slowly.

"I went back to Rainy Butte once. Did I ever tell you that?" he asked me.

"Not really."

"My father said to me, "Don't be afraid of what you see up there on the mesa."

Bluejay sipped herbal tea and continued.

"The horse came out of the sun with a mane of sunrays and rainbows. A circle of golden pollen surrounded his head. I knew right away this was the Sun Father's horse.

"He galloped at me, hooves pounding, echoing on the clouds. Don't be afraid, don't be afraid. I took a deep breath and held it in me for all I was worth. The great horse kept coming.

"I closed my eyes and the horse passed through me. After that, a gentle rain came down. I knew then I would always be a horseman like my father before me and his father before him, all the way back to the beginning. We have a saying—

> The horse
> Of the sun
> Belongs to me
> On this day
> But tomorrow
> He will belong
> To another

Eleven

Gila Monster

Over time, I learned that if the storyteller is a medicine man, his powers come from the very first one. The first teller.

So the gift of telling comes down through the ages. That is what the Navajo practitioners say. That is what Bluejay says, and what he told me so many years ago.

He gave me the following instructions:

"You must sprinkle sacred pollen in four directions. Then you pray for the protective armor, the hard scales that shield the ancient lizard of beginnings, *Pichiquatay*.

"You sing the songs of flint. The songs of power. You rub the devil's claw, cat's claw, willow bark, rose petal, skullcap on your "hurt places" and you pray for a sacred vision."

Bluejay went on with his story:

"I have had many of these sacred ceremonies since my own early curing lessons. And this that I am about to tell you comes from The Flintway, a gift from Gila Monster."

"First I do deep breathing with Sacred Datura. But sometimes I use morning glory, boiled first to remove the poisons, then imbibed as a tea."

I told Bluejay that once I asked for a sign. That was when I found a Blue-Eyed-Bear talisman under my wife Laura's left foot.

The next day, when I looked at the turquoise wedding ring I have worn for so many years, Laura's face appeared on the band. Then I heard the song of healing that Bluejay bestowed, and it went like this:

Black Ant People
restore this broken man
bring every part of him back
so that he is no longer
broken

Walking
in beauty, Ant People
come and sing the song of Thunder.

Let Rainbow come in
and give his blessing

Lift the shattered man—
make him perfect again.

Let Sun Looking
Moon Looking
Mountain Looking
give their blessing

Let
Sun
Moon
Woman
Mountain
Happiness
Enter the hurt heart

Hail Chanter

And let all be one
with Sun and Moon
and Black Wind
go under your feet

Let White Wind go
beneath you

Let Sun go into
Glittering Wind
and make Whirlwind
bless all

Make a man walk again

Let Spider People
start him off

These were the words
Half Chest heard
in his dream of sleep
in his wandering
journey back to beauty.

Let Talking God know,
let Great Grandfather
place body and song
together as one

Twelve

Waterway

Sometime after this, I learned more about the healing ceremony and how it travels from the first world of darkness to the second world, and then to the upper worlds of light.

The hero of the tale moves through the watery womb of Mother Earth into the upper dimension of the Sun Father's light.

Storytellers say: "Man of First Earth raised himself up like corn, and as it rained for four days, the corn plant whose form resembles a human figure with arms and legs, just grew, and grew."

I told Bluejay that I was once trapped by an octopus and learned the lesson of The Waterway through personal experience.

This may seem as far from the dry lands of the Navajo as one could get. But it is not unlike the myth of Water Monster in the ceremonial rite of The Waterway. It is where the hero, a man of First Earth, is taught the power of water by almost drowning.

Such was my experience on an Antiguan reef, and it is not something I will ever forget.

The octopus captured my wrist and pinned me against a buttress of coral. My snorkel was a half-inch from the surface of the sea. But I was out of reach of air. I was drowning. I escaped by letting go my life. Just as First Man did with Water Monster. The moment I released myself, the octopus did the same, and I floated to the upper air, the sunlight and reclaimed my life.

Finding the Rainbow Path

*The Man of First Earth
met Lightning who gave him
a new name: Thunder Boy
And together, they followed Gray Heron and
crossed
Black Peak Rocks
Straight Lightning Path
Crystal Path, Rainbow Path
until they reached
the edge of the Sky
where they met
Dry Web Spider
where the wind was loud
But Spider's house held
And does to this day.*

Thirteen

Windway

Tony Hillerman once spoke to me about a man who asks his Navajo friend to build some fences for him over by Redondo Mesa.

His friend agrees, but when he's told to look out for rattlesnakes on the lava rocks, he says, "Snakes are friends of the Navajo."

A little later, the landowner sees many dead rattlers around the neatly strung fence wire. "I thought you said the rattlesnakes and the Navajo were friends…"

"Well, the worker said, "A man can have too many friends."

A few years later, my brother was rattler-bitten. He wanted to make a belt out of a diamondback he saw by the railroad track. "I almost died," he told me, "not from the snake venom, which gave me an unusual visionary experience, but from the anti-venin which lowered my blood pressure to the edge of death. I survived, but it was a close call."

To my knowledge he has not killed another snake. Bluejay, hearing this story, explained that in The Windway ceremony the power of Great Snake is helped by Lightning, Thunder and, most importantly, Wind.

"How do you guard against offending Great Snake?"

Bluejay said, "The snake has the power of Thunder and Lightning. If you eat an animal not freshly killed or if you ignore the dominion of Great Snake, you could get other illnesses including heart trouble."

He also explained that in curative sandpainting, Lightning comes out of Great Snake's mouth. This is his power. Further, Great Snake is a link, a cohesion between Earth and Sky.

Feathered Serpent—part bird, part snake—represents this ancient union. And in Navajo sandpaintings, the marks on Great Snake's back depict deer tracks (symbols of a fleet-of-foot, yet earthbound animal) Yet one who can fly like the wind.

In the myths I have noticed that Little Wind is an informer, a gentle messenger, while Big Wind is an aggressive warrior. When Elder Brother violates Great Snake's domain, he is punished "terribly" as he himself says. By summoning and praying to The Wind People, who breathe Life into his fingers, Elder Brother is healed.

In the code of Great Snake, the lesson must be learned—obey the code, be humble, show no fear. Do not go where you are not wanted. Live in harmony with Snake, Wind, Thunder and Lightning and walk upon The Path of Rainbow harmony.

When I was struck by lightning—I was on a singular path: "I and I alone walk this earth." I was not one with the All, as the Navajos preached to me.

Now, Elder Brother and I are mystic brothers with all the other members of The Windway, The Waterway, and Flintway.

Fourteen

Coming of the Sun

Bluejay wasn't the only one who told me stories that related to my life, and my "lightning strike".

Other friends were Ray Tsosie, Jimmy Blue-Eyes and Ronnie Brown, who once said, "You can only be born Navajo." But Ray Brown said he did not agree. He said, while I was still in the hospital that there was a ceremony that that might work for me. He went on to tell me that sometimes when a person "falls from grace" as he put it, that grace can be sought and found again.

I told him, "Ray, I think that is what I have been reclaiming as Bluejay tells me his own healing stories. He has dropped me into a few of them."

"Maybe we can put you into more of them. Come with us to Starvation Peak and we'll show you."

I wasn't up to it, I explained.

He then told me the tale of Quills.

"He went up there to Starvation Peak in a bitter autumn wind and Quills was told to take off all his clothes He did this. The others grabbed some sticks and formed a gauntlet and told Quills to run between them.

Once again, he did what he was told to do. The Navajo boys beat Quills four times through the gauntlet until he was black and blue.

The last time I saw Quills was about forty years ago. He had a big smile on his face, and he took off his shirt with great pride and said, "I am Navajo."

I said, "You should have gone off with Woodpecker. Then you could say, "I am pecker."

"I don't get it," he said.
"Neither do I."

***

"There is no ceremony to become what you are not." Bluejay said this after I told him about Quills and Ray's time with him on the mountain of Bitter Wind.

He went on. "You can be shaken, bitten, frozen and moved to tears but in the end, you are what you are."

I laughed. "You are going back on yourself. You said there was a way."

"That way," Ray said, "is acceptance."

Fifteen

Hummingbird, the Medicine Man

I asked Ray Brown if there was a story that somehow measured up to some kind of medicine for a non-Indian, a storytelling apprentice.

He didn't tell me there was or wasn't such a story, but he said, "There is one about a little bird. A little blue bird."

I said, "Please tell me."

Ray nodded and this is what he said:

"A long time ago the birds came together in council to appoint a medicine man. They sat in a circle around Big Pine.

The warblers, the mockingbirds, the yellow birds, the blackbirds, the bluebirds, and the hummingbird.

"We need someone to take care of us when we get sick," said Blackbird. Now as everyone knows, Hummingbird knows all of the beautiful flowers, the herbs, and the grasses. He spends his life dipping into blossoms and sucking out honey with his pointed bill. *Hasteen Yazzi*, the other birds call him, which in Navajo means Little Fellow. True enough, he is very small, but he is also wise.

After much chattering, all of the birds agreed that Hummingbird was the most learned, even if he was the smallest, and they appointed him to be Medicine Man.

Hummingbird dashed about on his delicate wings with enormous pride; he sucked out the juices of many plants to make medicine. Then he flew to the mountains, and there he gathered the cups of acorn nuts, which he stored with the medicines in a hole in Big Pine, his home.

Hail Chanter

Soon, Blackbird, Yellowbird, Mockingbird and Warbler came to visit him. Between them was Bluebird, who was too sick to fly. He was sitting in his nest, which the other birds, carried between them.

Here is your first patient," they said. "Bluebird is sick."

Hummingbird fluttered over the nest. "Call our friends together. At dawn we shall have a sing," he said.

The four birds flew up into the sky, and when the dawn light came, birds of all kinds flew down to Big Pine. Black Birds, Yellowbirds, Warblers, and Mockingbirds made a circle around Bluebird.

At the break of day, they began to chant and pray; each sang his own song, except for Mockingbird who sang a little of everyone else's song, since he did not have one of his own. What warbling and singing!

Hummingbird sat in the middle of the circle beside the nest, looking no larger than a moth. Before him, he set 32 acorn cups filled with medicines. In his hand, he held the red flower which is like sacred corn pollen to the birds. He shook it gently over Bluebird and every once in a while, he gave the patient a drink from an acorn cup.

For four days the birds came at dawn, settled in a great circle around sick Bluebird, and sang. For four days Hummingbird shook the red flower over his head and gave his patient medicines. At dawn of the fourth day Bluebird hopped out of his nest and was well again.

"I am cured," he sang. At sunrise he flew into the blue sky singing the song of the bluebirds.

The others flapped their wings in excitement. "Hummingbird is a fine medicine man," they said, and ever since that day they have called on Hummingbird to cure their diseases. At the break of day you can always hear birds singing for one of their sick friends.

Old Navajo medicine men tell how their fathers used the song of Hummingbird for a prayer over their own sick ones. But now the old prayers are forgotten, and only Hummingbird remembers the words to the song."

***

With the story over, I pressed Ray to tell me more.

"I can't do that," he said.

"Why?"

"Because I am running out of time."

I felt strange when he said this. "Are you all right?" I asked.

"I don't rightly know," he said. Then, "I've got to go now."

A month later, Ray and his wife, Ethel, were killed in a car crash.

One day, after this happened, a small bluebird landed on my shoulder. It pecked me once on the earlobe.

From that time, I have had a strong feeling that there is but one thing you can do: Stay alive.

And one other thing Ray had told me: "Believe."

Sixteen

Bear

If you look carefully, "Ray Brown had said, "you will find tracks—five toes with claws."

I had to laugh because this sounded like the introduction to Ray's Werewolf, or Skinwalker story. The one where his wife's pants ripped in back and the wolf saw her bare butt.

"That," Ray commented, "is against our rules—to see someone's wife's privates."

"We are off track," I said. "And I don't mean, a bear track."

Ray pushed the long blue-black forelock out of his eyes.

"OK," he agreed. "What was what you wanted to know?"

"How do we catch the bear that broke into our house and made off with our children's turquoise jewelry is what I was asking about."

Ray chuckled. "Call the Natural Resources Council and tell them you had a bear butt break-in. "Or, if you prefer, look out back and find Bear's track, make a mold, and take it to the cops. They'll know what to do."

He was spot-on, as usual. I neglected to call the NRC, but I crawled around behind our adobe house and, sure enough, there were the tracks. Five toes with claws. And I remembered the old ceremonial poem.

Inside the hogan
colored earths make bear tracks
leading in,
bear tracks and sunlight—
sun dogs

at the four quarters.
Bear is soaked in sunlight
in the center.
Twigs at the entrance of Bear's den
are trees.

The sick person has a vision of Bear
when he sits upon painted sand.
Then Bear-man
rushes into the hogan,
snarling and growling.
The sitting people join in—
and Bear settles down
and grows quiet.

Four months later, using clay molds and the feet of the thief as evidence, the cops caught "the elusive, jewelry-stealing bear".

And he turned out to be an old fat white man with unshorn toenails and three spare tires around his waist. He'd stolen the cherished jewelry and sold it in Santa Fe.

When Bluejay dropped by, he told Laura and me there was an ancient story about a Navajo theft that went back hundreds of years. A story that went back to Daylight People and Night People, who once had a race. Bear, being day-stalking and night-preying could've gone on either side, but he figured the Night People, like Bat, Owl, and Coyote would serve him best as thief partners."

I poured Bluejay another cup of chamomile herbal tea and he went on to say this: "Bear wanted to win the race so bad, he put each of his moccasins on the wrong foot."

"And that—"

"Lost the race for all the Night animals," I finished, and Bear's been on their bad list ever since that time. I am just guessing, but isn't that how the old tale goes?"

Bluejay nodded, "yes you got that right. The bear thief of yours, was a loser twice over."

"How do you figure?"

"He was a white man and he needed to trim his toenails."

***

I found out later that Navajos used the ceremonial Mountain Top Way to get rid of Bear's thieving ways. Worse, Bear's a *cougher*. If you go out on the trail at night, you'll hear what I mean. Coughs and bad luck and an alliance with dark deeds make Bear a tough customer, a terrible trail-walker, especially if you are up on Black Mountain where some really bad bears make their home.

It was after Bluejay's visit that we finally accepted the turquoise loss. "You have a Pueblo pot full of parrot feathers," he pointed out. "Back on the reservation these are worth a lot of money. Particularly, the red, gold, green and blue."

He was right. Even our parrot, George, steals his own feathers, the prettiest feathers you've ever seen. And if I should ever go to a track meet without my old felt Stetson, glorified by George's tail-feathers, I'd have fewer Navajos sitting by me.

My "George feathers" tucked into the horsehair hat band got me more friends from the Rez than I would have otherwise.

Bluejay likes to say, "You and your parrot don't just talk to each other, you argue over which feathers go where!" I couldn't argue with that logic.

Seventeen

Hozhoni

So the Holy People prayed over caterpillar and he turned into butterfly. And he flew to the Mountain-Where-Flint-Is-Kept. After gathering four flints he returned to the Holy People and put the flints into the hooves of the horse. The great horse stirred, and came to life. Then he surged, struck the air with his hooves and galloped into the clouds. This is why the tracks of a horse look like the wings of a butterfly.

It was almost morning.

He rode into it and a hummingbird hung in the air before his face. He looked up and saw the moon was fading but still present in the sky. As he rode on he saw what looked to be a vision—a pair of silver spurs hanging from a juniper bough.

He did not know what that could mean and he sang the morning prayer of Hozhoni, which made him feel better.

May all be well above me
May all be well below me
May all be well all around me
The sky, be well
The earth, be well
The light, the darkness
The mystery that is fire
The prayer that is water
In harmony it is done

Hail Chanter

In harmony it is finished
May harmony be all round me
All the days of my life

Memory brought it back: the old trail of his childhood, up the foot of Rainy Butte.

Tying his horse to a tree, he took the rest, walking. The climb was much harder than he remembered. His legs were older, less sure, more easily tired. As he climbed upward, he blessed his legs, his feet, his boots. And, climbing, kept going up, one step at a time.

What he found was this: He still knew the trail that went back into himself. The jagged rocks, the slippery jointed cracks, the slick cobble, the falling off places.

At the top of Rainy Butte he prayed again.

I walk in plain sight of my home
I am at the entrance of my home
I am in the middle of my home
I am at the back of my home
I am at the top of the pollen footprint
Before me it is beautiful
Behind me it is beautiful
Under me it is beautiful
Above me it is beautiful
All round me it is beautiful

Now he felt himself rising and expanding with the prayer, as he became a part of everything around him. He felt the world echo with this expansion. The brightness all around him turned brighter.

And something happened.

His father's words came back to him.

"Don't be afraid of what you see up there."

Then the horse came suddenly out of the sun.

A golden horse with a mane of sun rays and with feet of flint butterflies that clattered on the clouds.

The horse came out of the sun and clattered on the clouds, and kicked lightning loose on the world below.

He trembled at the sight of it.

The horse came right at him, nostrils flaring, a halo of pollen shining around the golden head, a song coming from the hooves, a dancing, wild, prancing horse with a wildflower hanging from one corner of the foam-sparkling mouth.

The horse galloped straight at him.

He closed his eyes, praying softly.

And now the horse was almost on him, he could feel the great creature's breath, the force of such a great, powerful body moving through the light of morning.

I am going to be crushed to death, he thought.

But, then again, his father's words returned to his ear.

He heard them and repeated them like a chant.

Then he closed his eyes and the horse came on and it was night in his head, and the horse still came on with a sunbeam in his mouth for a bridle. He wanted to dive down and flatten himself or make himself so small he was an ant person.

But he held tight to his father's words.

And he released his fear.

And the great horse of the sun passed lightly through him.

He felt the horse enter him, go through him, go beyond him.

Then he opened his eyes.

Hail Chanter

Now the horse was already down to the foot of Rainy Butte.

He saw the gold-white of the horse's tail, a cloud of dust rising in the wake of the horse's thunder.

After the beautiful horse was gone, a gentle rain came, and he sang the song of Sun Father's horse:

Hear his whinny now
The horse of heaven,
Sun Father's horse

See him feed on flowers now
The horse of the Sun
Whose butterfly hooves
Dance upon a cloud

Watch him disappear now
Sun Father's horse
Into the mists of holy pollen

Hidden, he is hidden
Hear, now, his neigh
Sparkling water falls from his face
Dust of glitter grains
Rises at his hooves

Hidden, he is hidden
Deep within us
The horse of heaven
Sun Father's Horse

***

Sometime after Bluejay told me the story of Sun Father's horse, he did a drawing for me of four sacred Navajo mountains. And he explained that the mountains were the four stages of human life. They began in the East, the mountain of birth, and they ended of course, in the North, the mountain of immortality. While Bluejay talked to me his son picked up his pencil and began to darken the lines of his father's mountains.

"I think he's going to be an artist, like his father," I said.

Bluejay made no effort to take the pencil out of his son's hand. Although, by now, he'd altered the drawing so that it had become his. Bluejay, seeing this, laughed. "There is the song and there is the echo. We like the echo as much as the song."

A few days later, Bluejay brought me a juniper root he'd found in Crown Point. It was song and echo in bird and tree. For he'd carved, sanded, and oiled the root until it was no longer juniper – just the supple, elongated head of a Gray Heron.

"My gift to you, and so now you have the savior of the Navajo." I knew the old sky story and how helpful Gray Heron was and I was deeply grateful.

Many years have gone by since Bluejay gave me the root-bound heron.

I believe in the bird's power to heal those in need.

My gray heron, carved by Bluejay, is wingless, but not flightless. An echo of juniper tree, ancient story, and long friendship.

Book Two

Eighteen

Man, Mouse, Bear

I am in here for two months, five days a week
All of July and August
If the devil in my chest decides to return
And haunt the space above, in back, and behind, my chest,
my shoulder blades.
Who knows what dark magic lies
Beneath the province of bone, blood and muscle
That we call a body

Even I, the patient trying to be cured
From a lightning strike that turned into
Breast cancer reminds himself that
His heart beats because of the radiation machines.

Every so often, during treatment time, one of the patients would say something like—"Well, this is my last rotisserie turn under the big broiler."

As for me, I would rather be on the Rez, enduring a four or eight day healing ceremony. But, today, most Navajos go to the hospital for cancer treatment. The "Old Ways" are not everyone's ways anymore. But be that as it may …

… I was thinking, maybe Hasteen Klah, the last priest of the Hail Chant, which cured lightning strikes, could help me with my breast cancer. But Klah died in 1937. And now, if there is a hail chanter somewhere, I don't know of it.

The woman opposite me was leaving St. Christus. She was done with her cancer treatment.

I was looking at her from across the room.

She seemed to be in the best of health.

That is the thing with cancer. It is a tricky devil. No one knows when it will strike, or when, after having struck, and been banished, no one knows when the devil will return. A doctor told me the other day that even the word cancer strikes fear into a person's eyes.

I envy the shapely blond about to leave the radiation waiting room. She's leaving.

I saw her packing up her traveling bag. "Leaving us so soon?" I said.

"Sorry about that," she replied. For a moment her green eyes locked on mine. "I really am. But I'm going on a walkabout now. Every day, another mile or more, until I am so restored I won't even remember any of you. And I don't mean that in an unkind way. I just want to be away from places where cancer is the main topic of conversation. I want to get to a place in my life where I don't even remember the color of this carpet or the drapes or those two little plastic dwarves under that rubber tree over there by the window."

"You can't get away from what you've gone through," a grizzled man said sitting near me.

"What happened to you?" I asked him.

He was in a wheelchair and the glistening chrome contraption where his right leg should have been glittered with menace, at least to me, who bore metal in my right leg from a motorcycle accident.

The chrome-legged man shrugs. "I lost my leg and my wife to a bear."

There was silence in the waiting room.

The only sound was the rasp of the old man's breath.

That, and the furious dance of a mouse in the outdoor back entryway of the hospital. I watched the mouse. It wasn't going to give up trying to climb the adobe walls of its outdoor prison.

The old timer who lost his wife to a bear continues. He knew his narrative had more power than an eccentric little mouse trying to get out of a glass-walled enclosure.

"Grizzly it was," the one-legged man mentions in a gravelly voice. "I was up in Alaska and the snow was still pretty much elbow deep if you went off the shoveled park path. The wife, she found a huge hole where the snow had caved in. I warned her to stay away from it. See, I knew what it was."

"What was it?" the pretty lady asks, hesitating at the door.

"A bear hole. The place where he holes-up for the winter." He took a deep breath, exhaled, and shook his head.

The mouse's patter-feet rattled on the entry porch windows. Leap and fall, leap and fall. It wouldn't give up. A cancer mouse, I imagined. Trying to escape its fate. I tried to think about how Dr Marcus would radiate the little furred-fellow.

"What it was," the old timer went on, "was Griz, all wintered-up and mad. He came out of his hole and ripped my wife a good one, tore her Levis right off her hips, then he came roaring for me cause I was right there trying to get the wife out of reach. But the bastard got me and forgot the wife. Took my leg off right here just below the hipbone."

"Jesus," a large fat man exclaims, standing by the mouse door.

The mouse was panting. I saw it quite plainly. Out of breath.

The pretty lady left on that bluejean-tearing note.

Chrome leg closed his eyes. "End of story, except the wife left me," he concluded, and suddenly he was sound asleep.

I missed the walk-about blond and tried to imagine where she lived. In my imagination she lived alone in a cabin in the high mountains. Healing mountains, far away from Cancer.

Bored, I looked around the waiting room. There was a man sitting across from me in one of the soft chairs that had a sign that says: Do Not Sit Here. He stretched his arms over his head, sighed and said, "One time when my uncle had a cancer, he was sitting just like this, like I am here, nice and easy and by god if his tongue didn't fall out of his mouth and land on his knee." He looks around the room – "It happened."

"Anything can happen," my nurse, Marianela, said at the door to the radiation chamber.

I smiled at her knowing what she said was true. She ushered a small woman into the sunray chamber.

I took a deep breath. The mouse was quiet, and I saw why. He'd found a hole about his size on the north wall of the entryway. For a moment or two I dreamed I was that mouse. Free, at last. I must have fallen asleep because when I opened my eyes, the grizzly bear refugee was gone.

I was sitting in silence.

I missed the mouse.

"Thank god he got away," Marianela said. "He was doing that for days."

A cross-faced man mumbled next to me, "Another minute I'd've got my gun and put him out of his misery."

"Since when is survival misery," I said. "That mouse had hope."

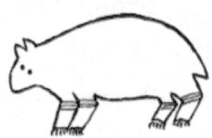

Nineteen

Tunnel of Termination

Dr Voltiano said, "If you opt for the genetics test, you may have a chance of seeing the tumor in your left breast. I've seen the sample, a charming little fellow about the size of a dime."

I imagined a tiny ginger root with little brown arms and legs. It had lived in me for a good little while, too, and I didn't notice it until my left nipple started to bleed.

But after the removal of this "tumor person," they froze it.

"Years from now, the folks at the hospital lab may find your cancer specimen useful for new treatments."

I mentioned my cousin, Kyle, who also had breast cancer, and amazingly, at the same time I did. "My breast cancer was the size of a pea," Kyle said.

"Such a small creature," Nurse Diane commented.

"Yes," I added, "but one with an inordinately large appetite for estrogen. That's what it lived on, Dr Wan told me."

Earlier, I was asked by Dr Wan, the head oncologist at St Christus, to raise my T-shirt so she could see the surgical work done by Dr Voltiano.

I lifted up my shirt while she ran her index finger softly along the scar-line that commenced at my right nipple area and went across my sternum all the way to my left armpit. "Dr Voltiano does neat work."

"She was indeed the artist," I said.

Dr Wan nodded, and a small smile appeared. "As long as you see it that way, you're OK."

Doctor Matt, the head radiologist, told me that I was "lucky Number 13 on the Oncotype Chart." He said, "Any number between zero and twenty on the genomic scale, shows how the cancer is likely to behave and respond to treatment later. In your case, Number 13 is pretty special. Pretty low on the return engagement list."

"I take this to mean I'm not dead yet."

Doctor Matt nodded when I said this, then added, "Those numbers are what we call a re-occurrence score. For you, chemo wouldn't be helpful. So you will be radiated by us for a period of two months, five days a week." He smiled generously. "We let you have weekends off."

"When will we start?"

"You are due to be fired-up any day now," and his smile widened.

Marianela entered Doctor Matt's office, and I followed her to "the tube room."

As she walked me down the hall, she remarked, "What you have, is as rare as a hen's tooth. One in one thousand men get breast cancer of this kind. Did you know that?"

"Doctor Matt mentioned something of this, just a while ago."

So now I was almost in the tube, as some St Christus patients called it.

"Remove your shirt, please."

"You want to feast your eyes on my artistic scar, is that it?"

She gave me a critical look. "You're not my type."

We both laughed.

I told her, "Doctor Voltiano is an amazing surgeon. I am proud of this scar. It's a little like the one my father had on his right shoulder blade back in 1918 when the Spanish flu was raging. He was drowning in his own fluids, so they cut him open and drained him, and it saved his life.

Marianela nods. "How old was he?"

"He was eighteen."

"Hmm. Your chart says you are about to turn seventy-five."

"On October 13 and that, by the way, is my lucky Oncotype number."

Marianela said, "Luck does play a part in this. OK, we are ready Captain Marvel."

Shirtless, I lay flat against the table pad staring at the mouth of the tube that was about to devour me.

The overhead light dimmed; Marianela stepped away.

The next thing I knew, there was a gentle vibration along my backbone, and I was in the dark womb of another world.

Was it the First World of the Navajo? Whose mythology I had been studying for more than fifteen years? I closed my eyes tight and …

… There was no sun, moon or stars.
Coyote was off somewhere trying to find the source of the dawn.
"Let's hope he doesn't try to steal Water-Monster's babies,"
White Hawk said.
But of course, considering who he was, he did.
And then the waters rose, and the Great Flood began.
It swallowed up White Mountain, Blue Mountain,
Yellow Mountain and Black Mountain.
The animal people gathered corn and seeds,
Bags full of earth and reeds in preparation for what was above.
From where I lay on a cloud, I could see Turkey scrambling
Down below and the tips of his tailfeathers turned foam-white
From the Great Flood.
Gradually we passed into the world above, but we had to squeeze
Through these skinny reeds.

Hail Chanter

Squeeze and squeeze until finally Locust
Shot one of his arrows into the lowering sky
And it broke through.

***

Marianela was there to meet me with a smile on the other side.

"You look like you went for a swim," she said. "The way you were moving your arms about. Tell you the truth, you almost set our machine off register with all that movement."

"I was swimming for my life," I told her.

"We are all swimming for our life."

Twenty

Emergence

The following day, I had at least a beginner's understanding of what the radiation paradigm was about. It was about getting in, and then out as quickly as possible, so that another patient could go in, while yet another was coming out, and still another after that, ad infinitum. Could it possibly be one hundred plus cancer patients per day? More?

I heard Marianela talking through the intercom somewhere near my head.

"You are coming out of the radiation tube now," she said.

And there it was back again, the world of light.

Marianela touched me gently.

"Wake up, Sleeping Beauty. You are back in our world now."

I rubbed my eyes. "Did I fall asleep again?"

"You were way asleep for three whole minutes."

"There's no sense of time in there."

"You can put your shirt on now. Most of our patients don't fall asleep. They come out; eyes wide open. You're a special case."

As I put on my shirt, then my shoes, Marianela cleaned the radiation bed for the next guest.

"So how do you feel?" she asked.

"Yesterday, I dreamed I was coming up through a deep cavern."

"You were," she said. "That was what I saw when you were swimming up into consciousness."

"But in this case, Coyote had stolen Water Monster's babies and the penalty was a terrible flood."

Hail Chanter

"Don't leave us just yet," she remarked. "We have to put more light into your bones."

"I was just arrived in the world of First Man and First Woman when …"

"Let me guess, you woke up!"

"That's right. I was sorry to wake up, I wanted to know …"

"… How the others fared?"

"You are pretty quick."

"I am Navajo," she said.

Twenty-One

Memory Babe

"So, how did it go," Laura asked me when I stepped out of the hospital doors into the bright morning New Mexico sun.

I was wondering who, and where, and what I was or wasn't. My dream of the Navajo emergence was still so strong, I wondered if it could have been real.

Maybe I didn't dream it. But Laura was ever my anchor.

And there she was, sitting like Little Miss Muffet on a stone bench under the portal (no one during this Covid time was allowed into St. Christus unless being treated for cancer.)

And there we were hugging each other in the flow of human traffic, going up the hospital stairs, coming out of glass doors, hobbling, limping, in wheelchairs and with helpers, and canes, and leaning deeply forward on walkers.

Laura reminded me, "You are no stranger to hospitals, Jack. Our relationship began sixty years ago at St Vincent's over on Palace Avenue, and you remember what that was like?"

"Every minute of it." I was standing there, hugging her to me, in a state of wonder. Where were all The Animal People? The sidewalk was dry and solid. Where had the Great Flood gone? Some fat pigeons flew overhead, and then a big-winged shadow went over us. Gray Heron.

We walked down the St Christus steps to the hospital parking lot. There was our Nissan truck. I wonder, for just a moment, if I can still drive …

Of course, I can. The moment I feel the wheel in my hands. But before I turn the key, I have a flashback to another time when Laura and I were together, and I was the one who couldn't walk without help. I remembered the heavy cast from my hip to my heel. This flashback was maybe fifty-four years ago when I was on crutches, like some of the people here at St Christus. Back then Laura and I were still in our early twenties, and I wondered if I'd ever walk normally again. Dr Kosicki, my surgeon, gave me no definite answers, just a very cautious, tangential, *maybe*.

However, here, and now, in 2020, I was overcome with memory.

Is that something triggered by the radiation I'd just undergone? Maybe.

I took a deep breath and told Laura: "I remember the old man who used to come down the hall in his robe to show me his daily urine color. He would come right up to my bed and show me the plastic bag attached to his catheter. He was so proud of the color that proclaimed he was still on the earth, still moving and breathing.

"Good old Mr Romero of Romeroville."

"An historic figure. A legend. I wonder now if anyone remembers there was such a place as Romeroville," Laura said.

"I recall how, one time when I was there in my hospital bed on the second floor of St Vincent's, Mr Romero told me of the big bare-knuckle fight in Old Town. That was the fight Jack Johnson won, defeating the local champ whose name I can't recall. It was bare-knuckle boxers back then. And they'd go 40 or more rounds in Old Town, right there on the street with people clutching handfuls of money for betting."

Laura reminded me that … "You had fourteen breaks below your right knee. I used to go up to the third floor of the hospital to visit you. You were attended by old-fashioned very short nuns with crepe soled shoes, and they all spoke in Spanish whispers." Laura smiled at that memory.

At the same time, the remembrance of my old hospital room came back into focus as we sat in our truck not going anywhere, just steeped in memory like a couple of teabags in a teapot.

I don't know if others hold images and sounds in their heads. But, sitting in our little Nissan truck, I heard the motorcycle coming out of nowhere. Was this in the parking lot or was I back in the Gallinas Canyon in 1967, with no midnight moon overhead, just the two of us walking along the dirt roadside in the dark.

No headlight, just the roaring Triumph motorcycle engine blasting out of the darkest canyon on earth – a cow or a kid or a college student (me) could be dead in a few seconds.

"He didn't know or care when he crashed into me. Seconds before impact I shoved you out of harm's way."

Laura said, "I'll never forget it."

"Nor me. I still walk with a pronounced limp."

"And one leg is shorter than the other."

"… And I wear my shoes funny, don't I?"

"The one on the right always has more tread, as if you are consciously walking hard on the left but not on the right."

"Do you remember," Laura asks, rubbing my shoulder, "waking up after the operation that lasted more than four hours, while I sat in those hard upright chairs on the third floor, and all our Navajo friends were praying over you. They prayed in soft voiced Navajo syllables. I watched them. There was Ray Brown, Jimmy BlueEyes, Ray Tsosie, and Ronnie—can't remember his last name but he was Hollywood handsome, and of course there was Jay, Bluejay, but we didn't call him Bluejay then, he was there, too."

"They were my saviors, those guys. I think there's only one left alive now."

"You mean of course, Bluejay."

Laura was rubbing my neck as we reminisced. "Are you feeling, OK?"

I looked into her lovely green Irish eyes. "I love you."

"I love you, too."

"Do you remember the poem?"

"The one I wrote or Bluejay wrote?"

"Jay just said it so simply. About there being no way to say I love you in Navajo unless you expressed it with that one word."

"What was it? Oh, yeah, I remember, *Ayo-nin-sh-na* …"

"… Which means, I said, "I like all that surrounds you, the sky over your head, the air that circulates all around you, the earth that is under your feet, all of it, that is what I love about you, everything."

"We're still together, Laura, so we must be doing something right."

Twenty-Two

Zigzag Lightning

For some reason the big tube is out of order.

Marianela took me to a smaller room and a smaller machine.

I'm not tube-wedged, there's no rounded ceiling over me. I am lying out in the open, so to say, shirtless and nervous.

"Let's see if you dream this time, big boy," Marianela told me jauntily.

I wonder …

With no camper's roof overhead, I'm not sealed in for dreamwork. But I do hear the funny buzziness of the smaller radiation machine, and Marianela and Karen put a soft heavy pad that goes from my neck to my knee.

Marianela winks. "Happy dreams, if you have any."

And I do … almost immediately the imagery comes on rolling like a movie.

***

I am back in the world of killer bees. On a ladder, lifting the shingles that need repair from Hurricane Charley. We've had some killer bees, but none have attacked, then …

I'm struck on the forehead, twice. These are the right-guard wingers that protect the hive. They hit hard. So hard my whole-body shakes. The ladder flips backwards. The two aerial killers, buzz off.

Laura laughs when she sees me. She thinks I am wearing a mask. Then she feels my face, hot as a griddle, and still swelling. Just above my eyebrows I have a true-to-life ledge of flesh and bone. I look like a Luis Guzman wannabe. Or a distant Boris Karloff cousin. Forget the imagery: I look like hell.

But I can still see clearly. And I can think. "Those killer bees have to go," I say to Laura. She says, "Anything that can knock a 180-pound man off a ladder and give him a face shaped like fist, has to go, yes."

In the next two days we find the nest. Helmeted and heavily covered in Northern Tool jacketry (rubberized and heavily quilted) several inches thick and made for hurricane performances, I dig deep enough to find the hide-out in the corner of the lower roof.

No one's there to see how much I resemble a Neanderthal, drugged on bee potent poison, heavy footed. I carry a saw, an axe, a hammer, and a crowbar.

And Laura gives the bees something to think about – smoke.

She smokes them out, I do the dirty work with the implements of bee war. Some sting but they can't get through the NT Jacket that is so many inches thick.

I sweat like a pig. The bees take a hike, just long enough for me to rip open their lair.

It is roughly six by six, all hive and honey, and the whole thing extending deep into our garage.

More than a day's work. Hundreds of pounds of honey. Three reinforced bags full of bourbon-colored beauteous honey that will have to be dumped because it is so dangerously peppered with live and dead bees. That, and the fact I gave them back some of their own weaponry – powdered carbofuro pesticide.

Laura and I drag the heavily weighted bags out to the road beyond the farm gate and wait for the environmental pickup. When it comes the worker pushes back his straw Stetson. "Don't lie," he sneers, "you killed these three guys and bagged the bastards, and now I'm supposed to take them to the dump."

I nodded, neanderthal-like.

He shakes his head. *"You better have that head of yours x-rayed, pal, seems like you got some bees in your brain."*

***

I heal quickly. But I never expected to be hit by lightning again—so soon after the killer bees had their way with me. I even found a dead, curled-up, baby bee in my ear. Then the storm came in and tore us a new one.

The bee noise died down just as I met a worse fate, arrows of lightning.

Twenty-Three

Tunnel Dreams

The dreams seem to come from …
    …what? I don't know.
    From the electricity in my brain, bone, heart.
    Driving home from the hospital, a poem comes to mind.
    One of the old ceremonies.
    Ray Brown told me of the hole in the rock.
    It's in Crown Point, among other places.
    "Don't go into it," Jay told me, and Ray confirmed,
    "because it goes far north into the land of ghosts."
    "Go there," Ray said, and you might not come back."

    The old poem writes itself, and I can't help but believe it is "Ray's ghost returned." Jay is still alive, but Ray's gone. Or is he?
    Anyway, here is the poem.

BEFORE

Before the deerskin legging
with its row of silver buttons.
Before the turquoise stone
set in heavy silver on the waist.
Before boiled mutton and corncakes.

Before Mexican pesos pounded
into rings and bracelets.

Before a child was lost among
the owl people and led home
along the cactus trail
in broad daylight.
His night-shaped eyes
blinking in the sun.

Before the hump-back
blue-eyed bear
was ever sat upon in a figure
of sand, a sand painting,
in a hogan ceremony.

Before night chant, mountain chant,
happiness chant, shooting chant
water chant, feather chant
bead chant, evil spirit chant
coyote chant, hail chant.

And before any chant under the sun,
Moon and stars ...

And before that, and before that
and before that ...

There was a hole that went into
the underworld from the above-world
of Crown Point cliff stone.

Hail Chanter

*Where the animals and gods
made their first appearance.*

*And after the fourth day of their
emergence a beautiful daughter
of one of the animal chiefs
was lost.*

*So that two searchers
looked long and hard until
they arrived at the hole
they came out of.*

*There they saw the beautiful
daughter sitting beside a stream
combing her hair.*

*Four days later, the two searchers
fell dead from that sight.*

*And that is why the dead
must never be touched nor even looked
upon, but rather wrapped in a blanket
and placed in an unmarked grave.*

***

Following this the hogan must be burned and the last footprints of family swept away and smoothed, so that the departed spirit can't find the way back to the living. Yet we the living must remember to honor all who have passed before and before that, and before…forever before.

***

I honor those friends who first honored me by saving my leg in St Vincent's Hospital and giving me back the gift of walking on two legs. I honor Ray and Jay, though Ray is gone and Jay lives on. I honor Jimmy BlueEyes, who said he honored my poetry of The People because it was honest and true to real spoken language. I honor Ray Tsosie who made me tickle him under the arm when my jokes weren't funny.

    I honor the two brothers who came down from the heavens to tell of the stars singing the star song. Some say it is the sound of corn husks rubbed together, some say it is the sound of small crackling fires, some say it is when white and yellow stars become igniters, striking fire by clashing flint knives against one another.

    Some say stars sing because they can.

    Some say they ward off evil.

    Some say they originate evil.

    Some say the evil ones are star-crossed bees.

Twenty-Four

Tongue-Tied and Tube-Tied

Somehow, this time, I feel the tube is too close to my head. I close my eyes and breathe deeply. Marianela is patient. I am nervous and breathing too deeply. She uses the intercom to say, "Why are you breathing like that?"

"Is it messing you up?"

"It's a problem. Too much going on in there. Our settings are coming out wrong."

"They call it Zen breathing," I tell her. "It helps to calm me down."

"As much as it helps to mess me up?"

We both laugh.

"I'll breathe more slowly,"

There are a variety of radio sounds, along with the usual buzzes, I hear a puppy whining and something like a large, heavy suitcase being dropped on a gym floor.

"OK. We are ready to start again. No more of that superman sucking, just do your usual dreaming thing."

"All right."

I close my eyes and Marianela turns on the radiation machine, and suddenly …

… I am five years old and down on the farm in Maryland. I woke up from a nap and there is Ray out there in the corn and he puts something heavy around my neck. It has a tail that quivers and a head that is cold. "How's that for a necktie?" he says, and laughs.

"It's a snake," I tell him.

"It's a dead copperhead, boy. Can't hurt you. I killed it with a hoe."

The gold and lavender necklace is heavy around my neck and sparkling in the sun and the tail is twitching and I am scared it will come to life and bite me and I'll be dead.

But Ray melts into the sunlight. The snake flies off into the blue sky and I am not a boy anymore, but a man and I am standing by a blue truck. My friend Jason is talking to me, the sky is dark, and lightning is flickering along the horizon and then …

… the whole world splits apart. One great wedge of pure white fire. The sky goes pink.

Wakeful, conscious now, I see Jason moving his lips, but no sound comes out of his mouth. The rain is coming down hard, but I can't hear it. The sound is in my head.

My body feels funny, shaky.

I turn from the truck and walk back to the house.

Laura is there and she says, "You don't look right. Let me feel your forehead." A moment later – "It feels like you have a fever. Do you hurt anywhere?"

I shake my head. "I feel all right." But a little later I am in bed talking to Dr Williams who says, "Sounds like you got hit with a sideflash. You're bound to have some headaches, maybe some chills. I'd recommend you go to bed."

***

Marianela stepped into my mind and mentioned, "Three minutes, Captain Marvel. The machines are off a little bit. Are you OK?"

"I guess I was dreaming as usual. This time I was down on the farm with the copperhead on my neck, then came the lightning strike I told you about."

"The one that Dr Marcus said might've triggered the tumor in your left breast."

"Snakes and lightning go together in Navajo lore."

"I never heard much of anything about that. But the old ones used to say the markings on some snakes, like rattlers, have lightning beadwork on them. Also, deer tracks. You hear a lot of things like that growing up."

"In the ancient stories, Zigzag, meaning Lightning, is an explosive snake in the sky."

Marianela laughed. "You're an explosive writer with cancer."

"I hope not to be."

"What? You don't want to be healed?"

"I want to be healed, for sure. In fact, I kind of feel that I am. How many more weeks of fire are left in my program here?"

"Four, I believe. We'll see what Dr Marcus says."

"The genetic test showed that I was oncotype number 13, which means, I am told, no need for chemo, he said."

She is wiping down the pad that had covered my chest all the way up to my chin.

"I was told by Dr Marcus that the likelihood of this kind of tumor returning is unlikely. My cousin who also had breast cancer said she was an oncotype number 23 and her doctors told her that her cancer wouldn't come back at all because of her upper-level number."

"I am going to call you Trouble."

"Why?"

"Because you are."

***

Leaving the hospital, I always got a good feeling.

Each day brought me closer to the end of the hot-house treatments. And the beginning of a new life.

Like when my father was drained of his disease, and as he put it: "I could start making up stories about how I got my big scar. I used to tell men at the gym that I was an officer up in the Carpathian Mountains, or sometimes, I'd say I was slashed by an Ottoman sword in the Crimean War in the 1850s. Once I said I met Florence Nightingale and fell in love with her. Of course, that was before I met your mother."

Hearing him talk and tell, I understood where my own poetry came from.

***

Laura was waiting on the outdoor stone bench. My own Florence.

"How did it go?" she asked.

"Between the snake on the neck, the lightning on the breast and Marianela's fire-breathing dragon, I guess I got a pretty good dose of white lightning."

Laura gave me a hug. "My half hero," she said.

"What's the other half?"

"The other half, silly. The one that makes you whole."

Then she glanced at the steps going down to the parking lot.

"What is that white thing?"

I knelt and picked it up. "An envelope with – feels like a card inside."

"Who's it addressed to?"

"Marianela."

"She must've dropped it by accident."

I went back into the cancer ward and asked Christopher at the main desk to put the envelope into Marianela's mailbox. "Found it on the stairs outside."

He opened it to make sure it wasn't something weird.

"Says 'Thanks for saving my life' —signed Yvonne."

Then he shrugged. "Who should I say picked it up."

"Tell her it was her old friend Trouble."

Twenty-Five

Itsiniklizh

You can't say the word in Navajo unless you are Navajo.

You can't say it any more than you can make lightning, or see a snake make lightning.

The Hero Twins, sons of the Sun Father, were trained in the use of thunderbolts, and they were instructed by the Sun Father: "Relieve the earth of evil giants."

And, according to legend, they did. One coming from the right, the other coming from the left. And thus the giants and monsters of the First World were eradicated. But …

Today, we can view the blood of those giants in the great deserts of New Mexico and Arizona and other parts of the Southwest. Those red sandstone wastes are, historically, mythically, vast stretches of dried blood.

And *itsiniklizh* (*ick-sin-ick-lish*) is the crooked, zigzag arrow that slew the monsters.

***

So, when I stand before my mirror, I am confronted with zigzag lightning. Sometimes, it keeps pace with my heartbeat. My lightning scar runs at intervals and angles, with a few smoky dots in places under and around arms and in the lower chest where the tiniest of all monsters – and the deadliest – cancer – thrived on a feast of estrogen.

How could this woman's hormone feed a beast the size of a dime? And make it grow strong enough to terminate the life of a man or even a woman?

Another way to look at it is this: all the tumor was doing was keeping itself alive. There could be an innocence in the way we look at it. Moreover, in medicine it is known that cures often come from the illness itself. So, cancer can cure cancer. But I don't mean to go off center with this, just to say that it is a complicated thing, as far as I have read and heard.

Recently I read that one of the earliest indications of the Plague was urine. Ancient Chinese practitioners asked their patients to pee near an anthill. If the ant people then swarmed the location, it meant that the person to be healed probably had enough antibodies to fight off the dread disease.

***

In my own research, a Pueblo dancing stick, so-called, looks like a thunderbolt. It is crooked like lightning, resembles lightning, and has bird tracks on it, a design inspired by eagles and other thunderbirds who carry thunderbolts in their claws.

I have been conversing with Bluejay, who explains, "Rattlesnake represents the earth; lightning is symbolic of the universe. When lightning zaps you, you then belong to the whole of life, the universe above and below."

"I believe I understand what you are saying, Bluejay. But am I one of the undead? Am I half-alive, since I was bitten by fire from heaven in the form of lightning? Am I like the lightning struck tree you once told me about?"

Bluejay chuckled. I offer him a cup of coffee, which he sips slowly as he considers my question.

"Have you been blessed by ceremony?" he questions.

"In what way?"

"In the Navajo way. You know, a lightning struck tree is a pariah. Something to be left alone. But, when blessed by a medicine man, that same scorched tree may be touched by a man. Once the medicine man has blessed it, the tree is thought to be holy."

"Heaven touched?"

"That's one way of saying it."

"Is a man like a tree?"

"Sort of." He sipped his coffee again, glanced out the window, and shook his head. "Things don't add up like that, not in our world. One thing doesn't equal another in measurement or definition. Things are just the way they are."

"I hear you. But is it possible to be expressed this way ... a man who is killed by a lightning strike, that man might only be holy if his body and the earth around where he fell was blessed."

He didn't answer and suddenly there was a muffled rattle outside.

Bluejay listened. He put his coffee cup down on the kitchen table and stood up. Then he yawned and stretched.

The rattling continued.

"Rattlesnake?" he asked. "Maybe telling me to shut up about these old tribal secrets." He laughed, I laughed, and we both shrugged at the same time.

Then it came again: the soft deadwood trill unmistakenly rattler-like.

Bluejay's face relaxed. "Probably just Locust out there."

Shortly thereafter, he got into his pickup truck and drove off.

Hail Chanter

After he was gone, Laura and I talked about the lightning, the snake, the way we perceive things, rightly or wrongly.

I was saying to her, "What we call Science with a capital "S" is stuff like this. Things barely heard, hardly understood. Mysteries. Rattlesnake, locust, lightning. Friends, enemies, healing ceremonies. These are all mysteries to those of us who think about such things and their possible meaning, lost in time."

Laura looked at me as she often does. As if I spent too much time pondering imponderables. Bluejay left. That was a statement all by itself.

"The wonder of it all, to me," Laura said, "is how a tiny tumor could cause such havoc in a human body."

"My mind goes back to the hired-hand, Ray Close, and the copperhead snake he hung around my neck. I was only five but I still remember that the snake's tail was wiggling on my left breast. That was my earliest experience with the universe and the earth, I suppose."

Laura chuckled. "You think too much."

***

Four days later, Bluejay sent me a message along with a piece of pottery and a poem.

The poem went like this:

I venture beyond the clouds to seek knowledge
Eagle plume in my hair to guide me
To the places of time
Rainbow on my right arm lifts me
My right hand embraces the songs
My left hand embraces the stories
Lightning on my left arm lands me

My feet leave imprints in the places of time
My journey is edged on cliff walls
To mark the time of places.

                        ***

I know I think too much, as Laura said, but Bluejay's poem awakened me.

Somehow, I remembered "The Song of Black Ant."

In the verses you learn that Elder Brother had entered a forbidden place, and he was instructed to turn back by the gods, but he didn't do this. He went on and was struck and broken apart by lightning.

It was then left to the Black Ant People to make him whole again. They sang the song of Light and Thunder, which, in time, restored him.

The song goes like this:

Thunder toward him rose
Zigzag lightning went into his mouth
Thunder toward him rose
Rainbow toward him rose
Happiness went into his mouth

And, as the song goes, Elder Brother is lifted up by the powers of nature.

It walks you
it runs you
it slows you
it draws you
it makes you

Hail Chanter

These words were once sung, they say, by Old Man Gila Monster whose armored body cannot be shattered by Lightning.

He breathes the glittering wind and offers a ceremonial gift to Elder Brother who is then made whole.

His helpers are a great many natural forces.

The Ant People, the Sun, the Wind, Thunder, Lightning, and Rainbow.

Not one, but all, return Elder Brother's life and limb, and heal him.

***

In hearing this old story, it comes to me that I, too, was the shattered brother. And I wonder if it was my lack of humility, just like Elder Brother, who dared to defile himself so that he alone could put himself back together again. That is the story. He went out too far with an obstinate belief in himself. He, and he alone, was master of the universe, he thought.

And so he was taught a lesson by the powers that be.

As was I.

As was I.

Twenty-Six

Put-Together Man

Sometimes I feel I am Elder Brother, the one called *Nayenezgani*.

The fighter, the warrior.

The one whose appointment isn't until 1:15.

Marianela isn't here today. Karen, her supervisor, tells me, "The big machine is on the blink right now, so we're going to put you under treatment with the smaller unit, all right?"

I nod.

Karen props me, pads me, moves my head this way and that, pushes my knees down, cranks me a little to the left. Basically, she is kind of flattening me so the robotic headlamp machine can eye me exactly where the tumor had embedded itself, where now, I have a twelve-inch scar. Karen has gentle, artful fingers. She can move me without moving me. I do the movement her nimble fingers indicate.

There is another oncology nurse, Dyanna. She is helping to straighten out my lower body. For some reason, the moment I'm flat on my back, I cross my legs. "No crossing," she warns. "That will throw us off center."

I uncross my legs and breathe deeply, Sufi style.

She taps me on the forehead.

"No deep breathing."

I nod. I am just a package of twists and turns, which is why Marianela said my real name was Trouble.

The lights dim, go out.

I am in the dark.

Dyanna speaks through the intercom.

Hail Chanter

"We're almost there," she says.

I can feel the rubber pad all the way up to my chin. Last time, something went wrong, and Marianela cooked me a bit, and I woke up with sunburn. My friend Mike had this happen once too many times, and he eventually lost his voice. It never came back. The cancer did. He lost his life.

I can't forget Mike. Nor can I forget these radiant angels who are taking good care of me, but this morning, when I stared at myself in the mirror, I saw a guy I used to know, me. This new me has a 12-inch scar almost from one nipple on the right, past the missing nipple on the left, all the way into the left armpit. I am a map of scars, lines going up, down and to the side, and all around. It's as if a tattoo master had his way with me beginning when I was five or six.

There's a notch on the bridge of my nose where Gerry chopped me with a WW2 sand shovel winter of 1953.

I'm a map of moving scars, which is way better than Elder Brother who was nothing but sheaves of shorn skin woven back together by a tribe of unselfish ants.

There are many more scars on me. The time I fell off a maple tree that was riddled with nail heads so some big stomp could clunk his way up top to a tree house. That time, I fell. Plummeted forty feet to earth where I lay bleeding for hours until my mom, doing dishes in the kitchen, recognized the leaf-littered blob that was her son, and called a doctor. In the late Fifties doctors still made house-calls when crazed little boys fell out of trees.

No stitches. Just layers of yellow sulfur powder.

Those scars are now overcome by the new cancer-removal ones.

I noticed knuckle scars this morning, too. Those are from a desperate ride on Cousin Peter's Triumph motorcycle. On this mad solo ride I went straight into a crooked juniper tree. Scarred me up nice, but especially my knuckles that looked like a bare-fisted fighter. I was proud of those badges of honor.

Speaking of motorcycles, in the late Sixties, I was struck down by one on a black canyon night in New Mexico. This time, the scars came from a hit and run drunk. He checked to see that I was alive, and flew off, and was not seen again until someone killed him in a gunfight some months later. As for me, every bone in my right leg was crushed below the knee.

If ever there was a time when Elder Brother wondered if the ant people could reconstruct his broken body, this was it.

He prayed. I prayed. My Navajo friends – Rae, Ray, Jay and Ron sang in whispers at my bedside. They sang their healing song.

> Black Ant People, come
> By your sense of smell,
> Go out and put
> Back together
> This broken man,
> This severed body
> Here are the feet
> Here are the toes
> Put them back where
> They belong
> Here is the ankle
> Here is the knee
> Here is the femur
> Here is the thigh
> Put them in place
> Black Ant People
> Put this Elder Brother

Hail Chanter

Back together again,
We pray you
Let this cover all
Let this be done
We pray you.

Twenty-Seven

Holes

Waiting to be radiated in the radiation waiting room is like being groomed for the healing rays. The things you learn. Just by listening. The people you meet ... like the woman named Mary with the hole in her left arm.

Medical science was mute on what happened to her except that cancer, the Big C, had eaten a hole in her forearm. If you held it to the light, she said, you could see clear to Taos 75 miles away. She was of good humor. It didn't bother her that not one single oncologist or cancer specialist knew how and why she got this cancer bite.

"I live a simple healthful life," she says. "No one in my family ever had cancer. I don't drink or smoke or stay up late and I always eat my vegetables. Why me? Why did cancer pick me for a bedfellow?"

Across from Mary there sits another worthy, a kind of man of the streets, a storyteller for sure. I ask him what got him to this place, the so-called rotisserie, as the drs call it.

The man bursts out laughing.

"Me?" he says.

"You."

"Okay, I'll give you the long and short, the skinny as we used to say. I was beaten up by Elvis' bodyguard. For real. Or should I say for reels because it did make the news. He was 400 pounds to my 168. I couldn't even defend myself against the man and he kept pounding me. I think that's what got me here for treatment."

Everyone in the room was staring at him by now.

"Look," he says, "that all happened a long, long time ago. Now's another story."

"Which is?" I prompt.

He snaps out of his bodyguard beating.

"Well, sir, I got BVD, PTSD, OCD, BPD."

"Is that all?" a large, heavyset fellow questions.

"That isn't the half of it, fellow. I am also bipolar."

Mary, sitting across from him says, "You can say that again."

"More to the point," the beaten man boasts, "I have a hazy left eye. I can barely see you people. When I squint, the right eye snaps into focus, then I can see pretty good."

"Maybe you should be consulting an oculist and a psychiatrist," the large man remarks. He leans forward and his chair squeaks from the weight put upon it.

I notice that he is sitting in a chair that has a hand-written note in big black letters: DO NOT SIT ON THIS CHAIR.

"Have anything else wrong with you?" Mary asks.

"I haven't gotten my Covid shots," he replies.

No one says anything, and he continues his ramble.

"Anyone here want to buy a car?"

No one says anything.

"I'll sell it cheap," he adds.

Silence.

"Look," he points out, "it's historic or histrionic or whatever you want to call it. The passenger door has a 38-bullet hole in it and I wrote in acrylic just beneath it, 'Ha! Ha! You missed."

This is greeted with a silence so hollow you could cut it with a mystical knife.

"I'm going to sell it cheap, folks."

Then he puts his face into his palms, and I have a feeling he's going to cry. But he doesn't. Instead, he says: "My kids love me. The cops won't arrest me. And, hey, you are still listening to me."

I smile at him and say, "Love, brother."

Then Dyanna comes in and says, "All right, Indestructible. Time for chemo and radiation and then you can go sell your car. By the way you never said what kind it is."

"It's an old beat-up van, just like me."

After he leaves with Dyanna, the guy with the waist wide as the Mississippi, says, "And I thought I had problems."

"What are you in for?" I ask,

"Radiation, like you, I guess."

He sighs. "It doesn't help being this overweight. The fact is, I eat a lot."

"So do we all," an even fatter man, says in the corner of the room.

"Yeah, well, I smoked tobacco with a pipe. I did plenty of *ciggyboo* and snort. I worshiped tobacco, tell you the truth. I even took a hot bath in it once. I used to go to sleep with my pillow stuffed with the stuff." He shook his head, saying, "and that's what got me here."

"Chemo or radiation?" the fatter fellow in the corner asks.

"Both."

"We are all in for it," I mention with a shrug. "And most of us will live as long as we don't get hit by lightning."

"Did you?" Mary wants to know.

"I did."

"But you're still alive."

"I met a man who was hit seven times and then he won the lottery. True story."

"You're next, Trouble," Marianela calls from the doorway.

Twenty-Eight

Two Travel Through

"The door on the right. You go through the little lab, and you're there."

Marianela watches me. "Not that door," she tells me. "The next one."

This is the big radiation/chemo room. It looks like the others, but it's bigger.

Once in the tube, as usual, I close my eyes, and when the "buzzinations" begin, I am out, flying free over the plains. I am with my student Travis Dailey.

Do you forgive me?"

"What? From the strike you gave me in martial arts class when we were working out with those Robin Hood poles? That was a long time ago, Trav. But I still have the scar to remind me."

"We are now swimming in red mud water," he says. "This way you'll think like a Navajo. Like me."

Immersed in red mud, we are so much the same.

For once, the same color, the same mind.

"Remember when you said, 'Rock down bottom don't feel sun hot up top?'"

He laughs, and tells me: "Rock, mud and blood."

Marianela teases me as I tug my sweatshirt over my head and get ready to leave.

"You were under for a couple minutes and change," she quips, but you look like you just saw a ghost."

"Ah, but I did, Marianela. One of my students from long ago. He was my student but because of this, he swiftly became my teacher.

"What are you talking about?"

"He struck me right here. We couldn't stop the bleeding."

I pull tight my forelock of hair so she can see the brown scar.

"I don't see anything there."

In the radiation bathroom, I take a good look in the mirror.

Travis' well-aimed scar is not there.

For a moment, I study my forehead.

No scar. But it was there yesterday. And all the days before going back to 1985.

Maybe I have learned my lesson.

But every morning after this, I search my forehead looking at that telltale notch where the wooden pole glanced off my head.

It's just not there anymore.

The mystic red mud and Trav's ceremony.

Twenty-Nine

Babe Ruth and the Ghouls of Mercy

I am now on my seventh week of radiation, and I have to say, there is nothing like it. Two minutes on the *rotisserie*, as the nurses here say, and I am out, thanking every white, blue and green coat in the hospital. For these are the bodhisattvas who save lives.

What amazes me is they never have a frown on their face. Their eyes always sparkle, they are never impatient, or perturbed, and I want to add that I love them as much as I love my own life. They are not separate from it.

There is a poem about these angelic saviors.

Ironically, the poem's entitled "Ghouls of Mercy" and it is written by a one-name Santa Fe poet, Rosé.

Ghouls they are not, the poet, aptly and ironically, states. They are rather the masters and mistresses of radiance who save lives every day.

Ghouls Of Mercy

The ghouls of mercy at the hospital
Devour the flesh to save your bloody life
Called from your chair there in the vestibule
They lead you to the laser or the knife
Or to the great machine, the monster eye
That sends a beam of radiation thru
Your every cell so it can crucify
That renegade and cancerous voodoo.

You lie down in position on the slab
The mask locked to your face to hold you tight
Technicians war again cancer the crab
That clawed and multiplying parasite.
Upon this field of honor, life and death
You thank the ghouls of mercy with each breath.

It seems to me, after six months of dealing with cancer and its removal, I am one lucky sucker. The radiant angels are with me now, whether in hospital, or anywhere I happen to be.

I see them now when I dream and feel their presence when I wake.

Another thing cancer has brought into my life is the Buddhistic awareness that we are all fellow sufferers on the road of life. That doesn't seem profound or at all unusual. But after lightning bolts, radiant treatments, and cancer battles, you see things more clearly in the city where you live.

You see, for instance, a man beating a bunch of cans with a stick while yelling at them as if they were miscreant children in need of a good beating.

You see a man barely able to walk and you imagine he must be quite old. Then you find out, talking to him, that he is in his forties.

You see, above all, the patience of those serving them, helping them, smiling at them, keeping their spirits up.

Sometimes I am almost proud to say, "I have had cancer."

Because, by saying that, I am admitting to myself that we all walk the same uneven, but always equally unequal, road of life. For it is as Black Elk, the great Lakota spokesman once said:

"Grant us the breath of life, as we have once known it – not as we know it not. We know that the stinging bee makes sweet honey, the worm turns into a butterfly, that frogs, once legless, learn at last what it is to have legs, that the rotten trunk gives way to seed, that the newborn eagle, all feather and fluff, one day will soar. All these things I know and respect and yet the change that comes in the moment is often misunderstood."

As is, I might add, the mystery of cancer along with the dedication and mercy of those who heal it.

Almost sixty years ago I met a man who knew the famous baseball hero, Babe Ruth.

The man I met had a toyshop and in it was a photograph of "The Babe". He told me that Babe "had a cancer." That was exactly the way he said it. "Otherwise, he would've lived longer."

I agreed with him.

"The cancer changed him. We used to go deer hunting together, and I would take the shells out of his hunting rifle, and he would pretend he didn't see it. But when we hunted, he really saw things as they should be seen, without the intent of killing anything. Things are pure and simple when you boil them down to the fact that everything wants just one single thing: to live. To be alive. When you get down to it, cancer is a great teacher. Babe had it and it made him better. Right down to the end."

Thirty

Bluejay

We are yellow corn mother and daughter
We are white corn father and son

We are the child of white shell woman in the east
We are the child of turquoise woman in the south
We are the child of abalone woman in the west
We are the child of jet woman in the north

I ask Bluejay if this lineage saved him from leukemia. Because I remember he had it towards the end of his time at Highlands U. more than fifty years ago.

He answers, "I survived by not dying."

THE MEDICINE MAN'S SON
He can serenade with Coyote
And dance with the moon, stars
& upon clouds.

He can charm rattlesnakes
And lightning, both at the
Same time.

His pet bird, George, not only
Talks to him, they argue.

Hail Chanter

To my knowledge, I have never charmed a rattler. But I'll take Bluejay's praise any day of the week. He captures the relationship of bird and man. We have had George, the Blue-fronted Amazon parrot for more than 45 years now. Time enough to get to know one another.

And it's true, we do argue. Often enough George says, "What are you gonna do?" at the end of one of our arguments.

Time passes.

It's now been fifty years since Bluejay taught me some of the Navajo Ways. He was a boy back then; he is an elder now.

I remember how he told me we'd be getting gray hair.

It didn't seem possible when he told me back in the Sixties. His hair was blue-black and mine was autumn brown. Now we are both gray.

He lost his front teeth training a horse.

He told me the story of Nuthatch who brought the first snow to First Man.

This how Bluejay described it:

"The people's hair was supposed to remain black. But that little bird person Nuthatch had a white head, and said, "You will soon be like me." When he flew away the dust of his wings fell upon The People's hair and then they knew there was such a thing as old age."

Then came Old Man Gopher and his face was all puffed-out in pain. Grandchildren, he cried, "pull my bad teeth for me." So, The People did as he asked until just the first two teeth of Old Man Gopher remained. They are there to this day.

And that is how The People learned about the coming of gray hair and the pain of sore teeth and the irreversible thing called Old Age."

Another time, Bluejay told me this: "We must keep on."

"Why?" I wondered.

Bluejay laughed. "So we can keep telling our stories."

When I tell him my story about how I had a little stuffed Panda Bear when I was ten and then later, a gray squirrel who saved my life when my bed caught fire because of an electrical problem, Bluejay chuckled. "Did that squirrel save your life?"

"He kept me from burning up by biting me all about the ears and finally waking me up."

A day later Bluejay gave me a painting of my squirrel holding an acorn shell with light coming out of it.

I still have it on my wall. When I look at it I see the other animals that saved me, one way or another. The centipede that crawled into my underpants. I told it not to bite me, and if it didn't. I promised not to ever harm a centipede as long as I lived.

I haven't.

Some days later, Bluejay gave me a small loom made by his wife Ethel.

"The rug in the loom expresses what we know – Spider Woman wasn't a spider. She was simply a woman who liked to weave."

There are so many twists and turns to all of this. "The humpback flute player, for example. He wasn't an insect, you know. He was a man who played a small wooden flute. I will show it to you one of these days."

Four days later he gave me a wooden flute mounted and framed. "I found it up on the Apache Reservation. They do the bear dance with it."

I thanked him and give him some parrot feathers. Red, gold, blue and green. He admires them. "These are worth a bunch of money on the Navajo Reservation."

"There's no need to wonder at the passage of time," he adds, "because our journey goes beyond the clouds."

Hail Chanter

"Every time I blow the tiniest parrot feather into the wind, it rains or snows" I said.

Bluejay smiles, shakes his head.

"One day," he says, "the wind will grieve for our songs, and we won't be here to listen."

Thirty-One

The Old Stories

It was Bluejay who explained to me that Spider Woman was not a spider, despite the imaginative mystery and beauty of thinking she was.

"What was she?" I asked.

"She was just a lady with a loom a woman who had very quick fingers, and a great talent for weaving."

"What about Kokopelli, the hump-back flute player?"

Bluejay laughed. "I have brought you a present from the lake at Apache country."

He handed me a small wooden box with a framed glass window in front. Inside was a wooden flute with four holes. "Could be that's the man's flute," and he laughed again. "They say he used this flute to set the rules of human behavior into the upper hemisphere, up in the milky way or the star formations, so that we might have a kind of permanence whereby we could judge disobedience on the human scene."

"Kind of like the American Constitution," I said, kidding him.

But he nodded. "Yeah, like that, I guess."

"So *Kokopelli* isn't just an old hunchback with a flute, he's a law-maker, or a law enshriner, or something like that."

Bluejay agreed with what I said, but he reminded me to look at the figure of *Kokopelli* that he'd painted next to the flute.

I studied it for a while. "So you're telling me that he is a real person."

"I didn't say that exactly. But look at the figure, the form of the man."

I examined his art more closely. "He's not a hunchback," I offered. "He's a man with a rounded back, that's all."

"You've got that right."

"One thing I told you a long time ago is also misunderstood. The People made all these myths, but they didn't come from nothing. They most likely came from Asia."

"I have heard from anthropologists that the Navajos originated in Mongolia. Do you believe that?"

He grinned. "Could be."

Thirty-Two

Healers of Hozhoni

Once in the Baja I was jogging at dusk and I looked over my left shoulder and a zigzag of white fire came out of the sky and struck a cactus about a hundred feet away from me.

The illumination in the dry, darkness of the desert was surprising to say the least. Then came the flame turning the arms of the cactus into bars of sunlight. But the sun was down, and the desert was in deep shadow.

I cringed to think what it meant, but I ran on, reaching our campsite soon after. There was some meaning there in the brilliant burn of the many-armed, thorned, bandit in black, and then robed in white heat of night.

It was still burning at dawn.

Some days later I was in Havasu in the Grand Canyon.

Nothing could, or would, happen there, I thought as I was still mulling over the lightning mugging in the dry air of the Baja.

Yet there was more to come.

A woman carrying a woven basket appeared out of nowhere.

She said not a word, nor could I hear her footsteps, but the truth was that she was there, walking silently up the trail by our tent. Laura said, "I can feel her more than I can see her."

"She wears a long shawl. She is heavy-set, an older person, I believe."

Time passed and finally she was gone in the direction of Mooney Falls.

Our Havasupai friend said, "Everybody sees her. It's no big deal. She comes up that trail each night."

"Is there anyone who doesn't see her?"

"White people don't see her. But if they're not awake sometimes they speak her language."

"You didn't say our language, meaning tribal, did you?"

He sighed and gave a brief laugh. "She speaks in a tongue older than this canyon. None of us knows what it means."

Like the zigzag in the dark, I thought, but didn't say.

***

After the lightning strike that struck me down, it was Kelvin Rodriguez, my qigong teacher, who helped heal me. He asked me if I was doing open hands on my heart. That's an old exercise we used to do in his class.

You put your left hand, open palm on your heart, and then you place your right hand on top of it. The heat this generates is surprising. Also healing. I did these three or four times a day for three minutes each time, and my heartbeat changed from sometimes-jittery to always-steady.

I have noticed that practitioners of such healing power are usually egoless. One such person at St Christus Hospital during and after my tumor operation was the oncologist named Dr Voltiano.

Every month or so, I would have an appointment with her, and she would ask to see how the scar was healing. She was the surgeon who operated on me and she knew what stage I was in, and how quickly she expected the recovery to take place.

Words cannot describe her fingers or how they worked their magic.

When Dr Voltiano ran her hand across my scar, I felt something that had quivery magic in it.

Something inexplicable was generated by her gentle, mystical touch. The merest movement of her fingers.

I could feel her touch long after I left her office.

***

As I stepped out of the hospital I said to Laura, "I am done. They say I am finished with radiation and the cancer has completely vanished. Look, they gave me a graduation diploma. It has fifteen doctor and nurse signatures on it."

We stood in the hot sun, once again on the stairs, looking at the document. "I've never seen anything like it," Laura said. "Neither have I."

We hugged each other, as people came up, and went down, and I was back on the high mountain sunlight of hope.

But, strangely enough, at that very moment – my right arm around my lovely green-eyed wife – I saw the face of my old friend, Charles Lovato, the great artist from Santo Domingo Pueblo.

It gave me a little shiver for Charles had been dead for more than thirty-five years. But here he was, pushing a wheelchair with an old man in it across the St Christus parking lot.

Charles was the one who had sprung his grandfather from the hospital. His grandfather was nearly a hundred years old, and he wanted to die in his own bed at home.

Charles told me, "I hustled Gramps out of the hospital and all the nurses just stood there and stared in disbelief as I wheeled Gramps out in a wheelchair while singing Geronimo's escape song, the one that goes:

Hail Chanter

In the wind I come
in the wind I go
in the wind
that is coming,
I come and go
in the wind I come
in the wind I go.

Yes, I thought I saw Charles in the sunny parking lot of St Christus, wheeling Gramps to his final resting place. And there I was, cancer-free certificate in my right hand, breathing the high dry morning air of freedom.

No wonder Charles, or his ghostly presence, was there just then. The wind picked up and danced around the parking lot doing a Santo Domingo prayer dance. I thought of Charles' book, *Life Under the Sun*, the poetry book he said I'd inspired him to write.

In truth I was his editor and even if it wasn't Charles and Grandfather Lovato climbing into the pick-up truck, I had my certificate of health, and I was going my own way in the Geronimo wind.

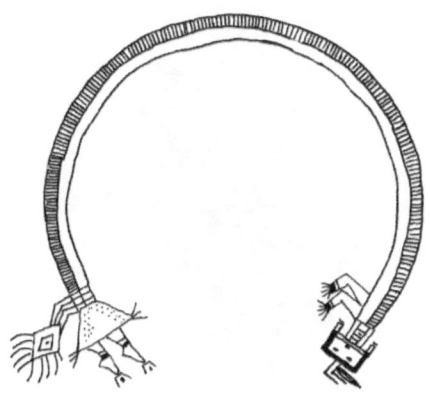

Thirty-Three

From my own grandfather I once learned that one does not need to travel far to find legends, mysteries, and prayerful magic.

As I sat in the sparkling, drifting snow, I thought of the Whimpering Chant, taught to me by Bluejay.

Far off, over the desert, I heard the loud rumble of thunder and Jay's words came back to me.

He sang:

"I see the holy wind and my brothers

Coming in all four directions, as they weep

And sing the Whimpering Chant."

So we become carriers of water in the desert. I felt Jay's words go deep into my heart.

Was I to fill the black jar of magic and carry it away with me? Bluejay had said in his quiet voice: "Do not worry about whose hands are on the sacred jar, "just carry it well."

And so, I began another chapter of my life.

Afterword

How and why I wrote this unending story ...

I started writing it in 2020 during the Covid epidemic.

My inspiration came from knowing the characters, of healing. They were naturally friends of mine, people I had known from the Navajo Reservation, roommates at New Mexico Highlands University beginning in 1965 and also neighbors who lived near our handmade adobe home in Tesuque, New Mexico.

I had many years to know some of them (a few were friends for fifty years), and to find out why they were traditional Navajos rather than some of their contemporaries who lived off the Reservation. It saddens me today to know that a good number of these brothers gone now. They have passed on.

I wrote *Hail Chanter* – to relive the memories, and to bring back the teachings I was personally given in narrative form by my friends.

In truth, all of them were what I describe in this novel – Natives who believed (and still believe) in what we call "The Old Ways". Many of their parents were healers, teachers, visionaries, medicine men and women who passed their art and practice on to their children.

***

Between Bluejay and me, and Mary C. Wheelwright the old stories line up pretty well as imaginative fiction, which is how I have presented it here. Also some of the stories in this novel came from texts by Hasteén Klah, who was the last practitioner of the Hail Chant. He died in 1937, so we don't know much more about the Hail Chant's origin except that, like most Navajo myths, it is a story that has its roots in the tribal cycle of disobedience and reformation.

The boy who is sometimes named Boy was, they say, struck down by Lightning while going down the San Juan River. Why, you ask? Why did a god strike him down?

Once again, we don't really know, but we can guess because it is said that if you do good, you are rewarded, but if you do bad, you are punished. Life does this to you, not powers from the stars necessarily, although that is often the case in the ancient Navajo stories.

Medicine people on the reservation often speak of disobedience, and how someone might possess too much confidence or what we generally refer to as ego in the culture at large.

In the transcriptions of Klah's Hail Chant, we learn that Boy has sex indiscriminately. That he is dishonorable because of this. Also, because his sense of self is very self-congratulatory. He is not really described as a perfectly innocent kid, but rather one who does what he wants to do when he wants to do it. Thus, the entanglement of the tale.

As Mary C Wheelwright points out, "The gods help the hero in his weakness."

He has a weakness for winning, too, we must mention. When he challenges Horned Toad to a race, he forgets, though he was told, that Horned Toad had much power. Therefore, in the race between the two, Horned Toad shot arrows into the Boy and this "made him ache all over." He also shot an arrow in his back and another in his neck. Then Horned Toad passed the Boy within ten yards of the goal, and won the race.

The gods had told the Boy (often called that) "to keep out of danger" but in this story he welcomes it, and so loses. And is, as a result, penitent and now conscious of his wrong-doing.

Hail Chanter

In the second race between the two, the Boy is given special powers by the gods – namely lightning in the legs to grant him great speed. Horned Toad puffs himself up like a storm cloud and makes rain so dark the Boy can't see his hand in front of his face.

Wind comes to the Boy and says, "You now have something to protect you against Toad's tricks. Throw down your Bullrush Hat." He obeyed and the pollen on the hat flew in all directions and blinded Toad who ran to Crown Point instead of White Rock and Grass Hogan.

Many watchers of the race felt sorry for Toad and so it was decided by the gods to put straight lightning in Toad's legs and Toad was told, "From now on we will be friends and not race anymore."

Roughly two hundred and twenty years ago, according to Mary C. Wheelwright, "When Navajos wanted rain in the summer, they would tie a toad with cotton string in a cornfield, and that would make it rain."

Today if you look at historical Navajo ceremonial art you will see that forks of lightning come out of Toad's toes. For me, the Hail Chant speaks from the past but it has much to say about the present. We are still in the race against nature, the race against time, the race against ourselves. Which is why I believe these ancient stories, which may have begun in Asia Minor, should awaken us to the deities of our own sphere in the here and now.

Gerald Hausman, Santa Fe, NM

About the Author

Gerald Hausman, folklorist and author, has edited numerous anthologies including *Tunkashila* which *The New York Times* called "An eloquent tribute to the first great storytellers of America." Gerald's awards include those from the American Folklore Society, Children's Protective Services, Bank Street College of Education, the National Council of Social Studies, and the International Reading Association. He has spoken at The Kennedy Center, Fordham University and on National Public Radio. He lives in Santa Fe, New Mexico.

Now Available!

AWARD WINNING AUTHOR
GERALD HAUSMAN

STAR SONG SERIES
BOOKS 1 – 3

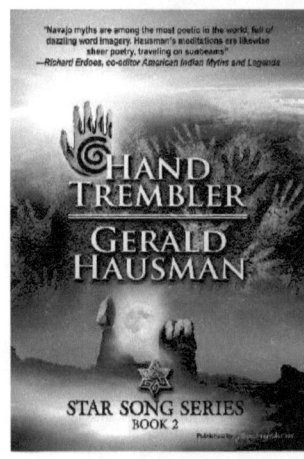

**For more information
visit:** www.SpeakingVolumes.us

MORE GREAT READS
BY
AWARD-WINNING AUTHOR
GERALD HAUSMAN

**For more information
visit:** www.SpeakingVolumes.us

GUNS

**This anthology with more than 20 contributors
from a variety of authors has something to please for every fan.**

Editor and contributor Gerald Hausman introduces the anthology with a brief history of *GUNS*. Stories range in tone from *The Momaday Gun* by Pulitzer Prize-winning author N. Scott Momaday, to *Choice of Weapons* by *New York Times* bestselling author Jane Lindskold.

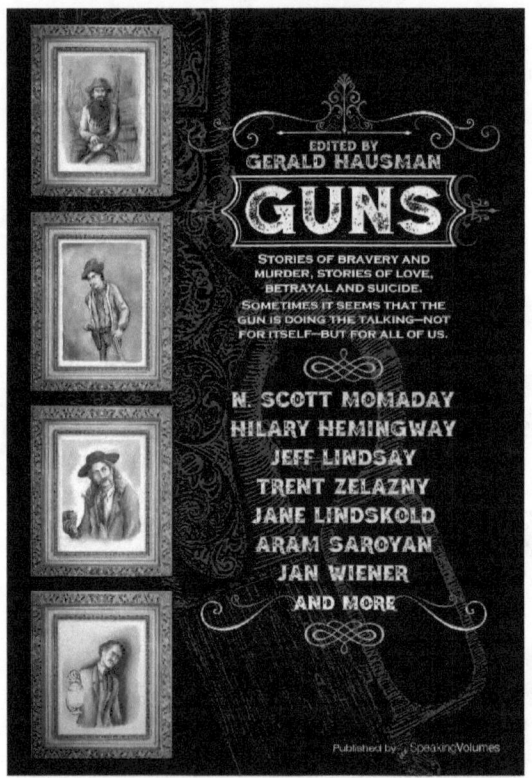

**For more information
visit: www.SpeakingVolumes.us**

www.ingramcontent.com/pod-product-compliance
Lightning Source LLC
LaVergne TN
LVHW041531070526
838199LV00046B/1611